Also By Liliana Rhodes

His Every Whim
His Every Whim, Part 1
His One Desire, Part 2
His Simple Wish, Part 3
His True Fortune, Part 4
The Billionaire's Whim - Boxed Set

Canyon Cove Billionaires
Playing Games
No Regrets
Second Chance

Made Man Trilogy
Soldier
Capo
Boss
Made Man Dante - Boxed Set

Made Man Novels
Made Man Sonny

The Crane Curse Trilogy
Charming the Alpha
Resisting the Alpha
Needing the Alpha
The Crane Curse Trilogy Boxed Set

Wolf at Her Door

PLAYING Games

A CANYON COVE NOVEL

LILIANA RHODES

Published by
Jaded Speck Publishing
5042 Wilshire Blvd #30861
Los Angeles, CA 90036

Playing Games
A Canyon Cove Novel
Copyright © 2014 by Liliana Rhodes
Cover by CT Cover Designs

ISBN 978-1-939918-04-8

This book is a work of fiction. The names, characters, places, and incidents are products of the writer's imagination or have been used fictitiously and are not to be construed as real. Any resemblance to persons, living or dead, actual events, locales or organizations is entirely coincidental.

All rights reserved. No part of this book may be reproduced, scanned, or distributed in any manner whatsoever without written permission from the author except in the case of brief quotation embodied in critical articles and reviews.

Dedication

To my son,
you're my moon and stars.

Chapter One

Cassie

"Breathe, Cassie, breathe," I told myself.

Wearing a pair of black trousers and a crisp white button-down shirt made of cotton, I hoped it was the perfect mix of educated, confident, and experienced. Unfortunately, I only had the education part and was losing my confidence as my nerves took over. I hated job interviews.

I grabbed my cell phone, my wallet, and a note with an address and the name of the man I was meeting on it. Holding everything to my chest, I squeezed between my daybed and the dresser to get to the bedroom door, careful to not bump my hip in the process. It already had a mean bruise on there. I didn't want it getting worse.

The room was barely a bedroom. Originally it was a small loft at the top of the stairs, but someone along the way had added a vinyl brown accordion door and called it a bedroom.

As I pulled the door closed, everything I was holding dropped to the floor. I jiggled the door to get the magnetic lock to meet and then knelt down to grab my resume, my cell phone, and the note as I pushed my shoulder-length dark brown hair behind my ear.

I folded the note and slipped it into the small pocket in the front of my pants. I had an interview that afternoon with Mack Draven, my roommate's uncle. As I picked up the rest of my things from the floor, my phone lit up and I groaned, seeing the word 'Mom' flash across the screen. I answered the phone as I rushed down the stairs.

"I can't talk right now, Mom. I have to catch the bus."

"What do you mean the bus? Is your car in the shop?"

"I told you, I had to sell my car to pay for rent. I have to go, Mom, I have an interview to get to."

"You never have time for me anymore. I knew this would happen as soon as you moved out, you've forgotten about your mother."

"I haven't forgotten about you. We talk every day," I said, sighing as I locked the door behind me. "You know why I moved here, Mom. I had nothing at home. I came to Canyon Cove to make a life and to finally get the job that I spent seven years in school for."

"Get a job? You had a job here. It wasn't good enough for your fancy doctor degree, so you left."

"How wasn't it good enough for me? I was there for two years even though it was the furthest thing from physical therapy. And I didn't leave that job, I was fired along with all the other admins when the company filed for bankruptcy."

"Still, you didn't have to go so far away. And now you're living with that stranger."

"I did what I had to do," I said, looking at my watch as I walked faster. "Crosswicks is a tiny farming town, Mom. There aren't many jobs there and I hated being an admin," I said, feeling frustrated. "You know all of this, why am I telling you again? I came to Canyon Cove for the opportunities. It's a big city, there has to be something better here."

"But you don't even know that girl. Couldn't you just get your own place?"

"You know I can't afford my own place. Not without a job and especially not in Canyon Cove. Plus Becca's nice, we're both twenty-seven, and we have a lot in common. We've become friends the past two months I've been here. She's the reason I even have this interview in the first place. I'm telling you, things are finally going to go my way."

"Well, there's a lot of money in Canyon Cove. You know they say you can't turn around in Canyon Cove without bumping into a billionaire. Maybe you'll find one of those wealthy men out there and then you won't have to worry about working. That's what your cousin Ashley did."

"Ashley? She's in Canyon Cove?" I asked.

"Yes, I didn't tell you? I spoke to your uncle the other day and got the whole story. She's married and has a baby now. I bet you could learn a thing or two from that one."

"I should call her. I haven't spoken to her since we were kids."

"You two were quite a pair back then, peas in a pod. Shame she had to move away though. She was the closest thing to a sister you ever had."

"You're right. I feel bad we lost touch."

"Well, it's never too late, Cassie. Especially not for people you care about," she said. "I'll email her number to you. Plus maybe she'll give you some pointers so you won't have to worry so much about working."

Sighing, I shook my head. My mother had a gift for controlling the conversation and steering it wherever she wanted. I loved her, but this was one of those times where she made me want to strangle her.

"I didn't spend seven years getting my Doctorate in Physical Therapy for shits and giggles. I want to work. And please don't start about my dating life again. You know I have my priorities," I said as the bus approached. "Dammit! I gotta go, Mom. I'll talk to you later."

I clicked the phone off and ran as quickly as I could in my black heels to the bus stop. As the bus pulled up, I waved my hand in the air, hoping the bus driver would see me. Just as I reached the bus stop, the doors closed and the bus began to pull away. I smacked the long windows of the door to get the driver's attention. The bus stopped and opened its doors.

The driver was a stocky old man with white curly hair peeking out from underneath his blue cap. With a slight frown, he squinted at me.

"I didn't see you there," the bus driver said. "You should have yelled."

"I don't yell," I said as I climbed aboard the bus.

I paid for my ticket and took the nearest empty seat next to a window. Using the reflection in the glass, I smoothed my hair, noticing it was already beginning to frizz.

The bus ride would take about half an hour. After the talk with my mom and the run for the bus, I was glad to have that time. Sighing, I leaned back against the chair, glanced at my watch, and looked at the old brick buildings as we drove past.

I lived in an area of Canyon Cove most people didn't talk about. They rarely even called it Canyon Cove, they called it the South End. The buildings were tired and old, and the sidewalks had buckled and cracked from the roots of trees that had been dug up decades ago. There were small shops lining the streets, all mom-and-pop businesses that were struggling to stay open. It was the kind of place that people thought of when they visited small, quaint towns, except time hadn't been kind to this neighborhood.

I found a room for rent in an ad online. Becca needed help paying the rent and I needed a place to live, so it was a perfect match. Then one day while I was scouring job ads, she told me how her uncle trained fighters, and it seemed like fate had brought us together.

Unsure how close we were to my stop, I checked my watch. *Dammit! It stopped again.* If I got the job, a new watch would be my first splurge.

I glanced down at myself and hoped I was dressed right for the interview. I didn't know what to expect, especially for an interview with a trainer in the biggest mixed martial arts organization in the country.

The Mixed Martial Arts Championship, or as most people called it, the MMAC, was the first and largest MMA organization in the United States. They started years ago when people thought MMA was nothing more than street fighting, but the MMAC brought it into the public consciousness and made MMA a sport just as popular as football or basketball.

As the blocks went by in the window, the buildings began to change. The old brick townhouses and storefronts became tall apartment buildings and skyscrapers. We were close to the center of the city, which meant my stop was coming soon. I took a couple of deep breaths and looked down at my resume. I closed my eyes and said a silent prayer that what I told my mother was the truth, that things really were starting to go my way.

***

"Okay, Cassie," I whispered to myself. "You're going to get this job. You *have* to get this job."

I smoothed down my shirt, trying to get it to lay flat, but the damn thing kept gaping right where my breasts were. Of course it wasn't doing that at home, but it was just my luck that it would happen now that I couldn't do anything about it. It wasn't the type of first impression I wanted the gym to have of me.

Looking at the wide windows facing the street, I tried to peek inside the gym and get an idea of what to expect, but I couldn't see anything. The windows were so steamy all I could make out were dark-colored floor mats and padded walls.

I pulled out the small piece of paper from my pants pocket and unfolded it to read the name of the trainer I was scheduled to meet—Mack Draven. I forgot things whenever I was nervous so I repeated his name over and over in my head. This was the closest I had come to getting the job I wanted after spending seven years in school.

I finally had my chance to stop answering phones for minimum wage. I had a lot riding on this one interview, and just that simple thought made my heart skip a few beats.

"You can do this, Cassie," I said to myself. "Mack's going to love you."

Taking a deep breath, I pulled open the door and stepped inside the gym. The scent of sweat and heaviness of the humid air smacked me as I entered. To the right were a row of stationary bikes and behind them were treadmills.

A couple of men in zipped-up nylon sauna suits looked up at me from their bikes. They looked weary and worn from cutting weight. Smiling at them, I walked further into the gym, hoping I could find someone to tell Mack Draven I was there for my interview.

Further into the gym, the walls had a dark blue padding that matched the floor. In one section, several muscular men were practicing their wrestling. In another area, a trainer was working on kickboxing moves with another fighter. Every man there was fit, muscular, and if the gym wasn't already hot enough, these men would have made me sweat just from looking at them.

Next to a boxing ring, a small man in trousers and a black cardigan with slicked back silver hair cursed at the fighters in the ring. I had a hunch that was Mack.

Not wanting to intrude mid-round, I watched the fighters weave and dance. I knew just enough about MMA to be dangerous. And from years of bonding with my dad over boxing matches on TV, I grew to appreciate the sweet science.

As the bell rang, the fighters went to their corners. Mack's fighter had a shaved head and was tall and lanky. Frustration filled his eyes as he slumped on his stool in the corner. Mack grimaced at him as he held a bottle of water for him to sip from. When the fighter spat the water out, it splattered and darkened his red trunks.

I didn't know how long their practice was going to go, but I wanted Mack to know I was there. The last thing I wanted was for him to think I was late for our interview, especially not when I got there early. I stepped closer to the ring and tried to get Mack's attention, but his eyes were glued to his fighter. Just before the bell rang again, he took the stool and stepped out of the ring.

"Excuse me," I said. "I'm here to meet Mack Draven. I have an interview."

He glanced briefly in my direction and snorted. "You can wait. I'm busy." Slamming his hand down on the ring floor, he barked at his fighter. "Ryan! What did I teach you? The right! The damn right! You've got no power! Step into it!"

He obviously doesn't want me here, I thought.

I folded my arms over my chest and thought about leaving. I glanced at the door then back at the ring. There was no way I was going to back away from the chance to finally get a job doing something I wanted to do. I clenched my jaw as I pushed my hair back over my ear and watched Mack's fighter.

Over and over Ryan threw the right as Mack instructed, but it didn't cause any damage at all. I studied his body, watching his muscles ripple and flex in his arm, when I remembered something my father told me a long time ago during a fight.

"Mack, he's not throwing the right from his body," I said as I leaned towards him. "That's why he's got no power."

His eyes flicked at me as he sneered. "What do you know?"

My first instinct was to shut up and not say a word, but the thought of working behind a desk in another office made me want to rip my hair out. I quickly changed my mind.

"I've studied the body, specifically mobility," I said, standing straight and hoping to sound confident. "That's why I'm here, remember?"

He snorted at me and turned back to his fighter as the bell rang. Mack climbed back into the ring as Ryan came into the corner and refused to sit.

"No, Mack," Ryan said, shaking his head. "I'm listening to you, I'm throwing the right but nothing's happening. I'm connecting, but I got nothing."

Mack's watery brown eyes flicked over to me, then back to his fighter. His head nodded slowly.

"Sit, you need your energy," Mack said, his voice gruff. "Tell me something. When you throw that punch, where are you feeling it? Is it here?" He slapped Ryan's chest. "Because if you tell me it's coming from anywhere else, we have a problem. If you can't get something like this down, you can forget about any kind of fight career. Use your body, not just your arm."

He shoved the mouthpiece back into Ryan's mouth as the bell rang and Ryan stood. Mack stood next to me and folded his arms over his chest, not taking his eyes off his fighter.

"You don't learn shit like how to throw a punch in school," he grumbled. "You a fan?"

"I grew up watching boxing with my dad. I don't know a lot about MMA though."

"Boxing's just part of it. You can learn what you need to. Becca told me you need a job, and I need some help. I have fighters who get hurt and I need help getting them back into the cage. Can you do that?"

"Definitely," I said, feeling excited.

"Okay then, if Ryan knocks this guy down with his right, you've got the job."

I nodded, unable to take my own eyes off of the fighters in the ring. They were just sparring, but I was still hoping for a knockout. With my arms still crossed, I crossed my fingers as I anxiously watched the fighters.

"Throw the right, kid!" Mack yelled.

Ryan threw the punch and I saw again that he was just using his arm muscles. By now he had to be tired and his muscles fatigued, but I knew he could do it, he just needed the right instruction.

Out of the corner of my eye, I noticed another fighter step closer to the ring. His body was covered with a sheen of sweat that outlined every contour of his muscles. His dark hair fell onto his forehead and he brushed it back with his hand.

He wasn't as built as some of the other fighters, but with his square jaw and full lips, he was much more handsome than most of them. I was having a hard time focusing on the fighter in the ring as my eyes kept darting over to the fighter outside of the ring instead. He had such a confident air to him that it made it hard for me to tear my eyes away from him.

He must have caught me staring at him, because a slow smile spread across his face. I looked away, trying to focus back on the fighters in the ring, but I had to see if he was still smiling at me. I fought to keep myself from looking back at him, but when I finally glanced back in his direction, he wasn't there. I looked around the gym, trying to catch a glimpse of him, but he was gone.

"This is the last round, sweetheart," Mack grunted. "Guess you don't get the job."

My heart sank and I felt my face go pale at the thought of coming so close but leaving not only without a job, but losing that job because I got distracted by some hot guy. I had to focus. The only thing that mattered to me was Mack's fighter in the ring.

I looked over at the ring clock as it ticked down. I was running out of time. Mack's face was covered in disappointment as he watched his fighter throw another powerless punch. There was only one thing I could do, and it was something I never thought I'd ever do. I stepped closer to the ring, knowing it was my only chance.

"From your chest, dammit!" I yelled at Ryan. "Not your arm, feel the power come from your chest and core!"

The fighters danced on their toes, waiting for the next punch to be thrown. The seconds were ticking down. I knew they were both tired and letting the clock run out. It was just sparring and none of it mattered to anyone, but it mattered to me. I had to get this job.

I slammed my hand on the ring floor just as Mack did earlier. I didn't care what anyone else thought of me at that moment, I only wanted the job. It wasn't like me to yell. No one who knew me would ever think I'd be yelling at anyone, let alone a fighter in a ring. But that's how much I wanted this job.

"Throw the right!" I yelled. "From your chest. Not your fucking arm!"

On cue, the fighter threw a right cross and it connected with his sparring partner's chin. The other fighter tripped backwards as I clenched my fists in front of me, but he didn't go down. Frustrated, I yelled again as my fist hit the ring floor.

"Left hook! Throw a fucking left hook!" I yelled.

I couldn't believe the language coming out of my mouth in front of all these people, but at that moment I didn't care. As the left connected near the ear of the other fighter, I held my breath. The fighter's feet crossed and he fell to the canvas. A wrinkled hand clasped my shoulder as Mack stood beside me.

"You did good, kid," he said. "You've got the job. When can you start?"

"Tomorrow," I said with a huge grin.

"Perfect. Take some time now to look around and get to know the place and talk to some of the fighters. Help yourself to some water in the lounge. Just watch out for the owner, he has a reputation for liking the ladies. He's around here somewhere, and you'll have no problem picking him out. It's easy enough to spot a suit in this place."

***

I spent the better part of the hour looking around the gym and its facilities. The place was huge and consisted of multiple gyms to keep the trainers separated from each other. From talking to the fighters and the other trainers, I learned that this was the main gym but that there were other smaller gyms. Not every trainer was lucky enough to train their fighters here.

I soaked in as much as I could, but the real reason I stayed for so long was that I was looking for the fighter from earlier. I didn't know what I would do once I found him, but I wanted to see him again.

Turning the corner, I entered a long hallway. Some of the doors were closed and had name placards on them. I recognized some of the trainers' names, including Mack's. At the end of the hall was a carpeted lounge with several café-style tables and chairs. A long couch ran along the wall. In the corner was a refrigerator and pantry shelves. Towards the back of the room was an open door that led to the showers.

I opened the refrigerator and pulled out a bottle of water as I looked at the time. I still had fifteen minutes until Becca came to pick me up. As I brought the water bottle to my lips, I heard a shower turn on. I couldn't help but wonder if that was where my mystery fighter had disappeared to.

Sitting on the long couch, my mind kept returning to my mystery fighter. *What if he was in the shower? Would it hurt to take a peek?*

It wasn't like me to entertain those kinds of thoughts, but all the sweat and testosterone in the air must have affected my brain. I tapped my foot on the floor as I took another sip of the cold water. I was at the point where I was trying to convince myself I didn't need to check the showers. I kept trying to talk myself out of sneaking in there, but my mind was already made up.

As I slipped through the doorway, my shoes made a soft click on the tile floor. I didn't want him to hear me so I walked slower, careful to not make any sound other than my heart pounding in my chest.

I followed the sound of the shower past the lockers. Each time I got near a corner, I peeked around it to make sure no one was there. Finally reaching the showers, I squinted, trying to see through the steam.

"Hmm, a dirty mouth and a dirty mind. Seems like you're my kind of girl."

Hearing a deep voice come from behind me, I held my breath, hoping to magically disappear into the steam. I didn't have to turn around to see who it was. I knew that instead of my finding my mystery fighter, he found me.

"I must have gotten lost," I said, thinking fast as I turned around.

He stood close enough to me that I could smell the mint shampoo from his wet, combed back hair. Knotted around his waist was a white towel. Beads of water rested on his sculpted torso and when he grinned at me, my eyes followed them down as they met his towel.

I forced myself to smile and look calm, but I knew I had guilt written all over my face. My mystery man grinned at me like a cat that ate a mouse. His dark blue eyes twinkled as if he was in on a joke I didn't know about. As my cheeks began to burn from embarrassment, he let out a laugh.

"I'll have to remember that line next time I'm sneaking around a women's locker room," he said.

He walked towards the lockers along the furthest wall and my stomach knotted. If Mack found out I was sneaking around the men's showers, I could lose the job I fought so hard to get.

"Wait," I said as I followed him. "Please don't tell Mack you found me in here."

He turned slightly, giving me a side look, and I noticed a smirk play around his lips.

"He gave you the job?" he asked as he turned around to face me.

"Yes, and I can't lose it. You have no idea how hard--"

He put his hand up to stop me, then stroked his chin as he eyed me up and down.

"Your secret's safe with me," he said.

He stepped closer to me, his eyes locked on mine. I couldn't look away. I didn't want to look away except to look at his lips coming closer to mine. It wasn't like me to let a man get so close to me that quickly, but there was something about him I couldn't say no to.

His long fingers traced my cheek down to my jawbone, then gently slid to my chin. I held my breath, feeling electricity from his touch that I had never felt with anyone before. He pulled my chin up as he lowered his head and his lips crushed mine.

My legs felt weak as his hand slipped into my hair. I wanted more of him. Opening my mouth, his tongue slipped inside and met mine. Gaining my confidence, I moved my hands over his wet chest, feeling the strength of his body.

The squeak of a door echoed against the tile and I pulled away, afraid of getting caught. With his hand still in my hair, he pulled me back to him and kissed me quickly one more time. He looked into my eyes again and just as I was getting lost in the deep ocean blue of his eyes, he grabbed my hand and led me to another door. He opened it and I stepped out.

"Get out of here before I can't stop myself," he said. "Mack will know nothing about this."

"Thank you..." I said, my voice trailing off as I realized we barely spoke. "I don't even know your name."

"It's Gabriel. Gabriel Kohl. And you?"

"Cassie Monroe."

"I'll see you again soon."

His lips pressed against mine again before he pulled himself away and disappeared back into the locker room. I leaned against the wall as I thought about Gabriel's lips and how demanding they felt.

Just thinking about his kiss was enough to make my head spin.

Taking a deep breath, I continued down the hall to a door that brought me back into the gym. Mack was sitting with his fighters on one of the floor mats. He looked up at the clock, clapped his hands, and the fighters got up and headed towards the showers.

He walked over to me with his hands deep in the pockets of his cardigan. His brow wrinkled as he approached.

"You feeling alright?" he asked. "You look a little flushed."

My hands flew up to my cheeks as I guiltily looked away. "I'm fine," I said. "Probably just all the heat in here."

"You get used to it. In no time you'll find this place chilly like I do."

I laughed, thinking that would never happen. I was always warm. I joked to my friends that it was my extra padding that kept me warm since it insulated me.

"Becca should be here any second now," I said.

"You a friend from school or from the restaurant?" he said.

"No, I answered her ad for a roommate," I said. "I just moved out here."

He nodded, and I could tell he didn't want to know anything too personal.

"Thanks again for the job. I promise you won't regret hiring me."

"I know I won't," he said. "I can tell you're a hard worker and you've got gumption, kid. Those things will take you far. Just watch out for the suit. Between you and me, I've seen plenty of girls get messed up because of that man. They think he's in love with 'em, but trust me, I know people and that man is in deep with someone else."

"No problem, I'll stay away from the suit," I said, shrugging. "What about any of the fighters?" I asked, thinking about Gabriel.

"Have at it with anyone you want, just none of my fighters of course. You'll be working with them so it wouldn't be right. You wouldn't want any of them anyway. Women weaken the knees, so I have a strict no-sex policy when they're training."

I looked at him to see if he was joking, but by his stern look, I knew he wasn't. It didn't matter.

If Gabriel was one of his fighters, he would have been there for Mack's talk.

Mack walked me towards the door as a black limo pulled up to the curb. A red pickup truck pulled up behind the limo and Becca waved from inside.

"Did you meet the suit?" Mack asked as he nodded towards the limo.

Gabriel stepped out of the gym from a side door. He was in khakis and a blue polo shirt that matched his eyes. Gabriel raised his hand as he nodded towards Mack and then winked at me. A man beside the limo opened the back door and Gabriel slid inside.

What? Why is he taking a limo? I knew some fighters earned a lot from fights, but to get picked up by a limo seemed strange.

"A limo?" I said to Mack as it pulled away.

"Bah, you know those suits."

"Suit?"

"Yeah, suit, you know, corporate guy. That was Gabriel Kohl. He owns this gym, the whole organization actually. Kind of young for a suit, don't you think? He can't be more than thirty and created all of this out of nothing," he said as Becca honked her horn. "Don't keep my niece waiting. Trust me, you'll never hear the end of it. I'll see you in the morning."

He smiled as he waved to Becca and patted me on the back, gently pushing me towards her. I couldn't stop thinking about what Mack said and as I opened my mouth to point out that Gabriel wasn't in a suit, Becca honked her horn again.

I sighed as I climbed into her truck. It was just my luck that the best kiss of my life belonged to someone I couldn't be with. I thought about the things Gabriel said, but Mack's words rang through my head. *He has a reputation for liking the ladies. That man is in deep with someone else.*

Not that any of that mattered. There was no way a man with his wealth and looks would want anything to do with a nobody like me. He was probably bored before when he kissed me. And as much as I wanted to daydream about it, there was no way I was going to be the girl who dated her boss.

Chapter Two

Gabriel

Earlier That Day

Sitting in my office, I was going over contracts for the next big event when there was a knock on my door. Glancing at the open doorway, I saw one of my main trainers, Mack Draven, waiting.

"Come in," I said, not looking up from my laptop.

Mack entered the office with his usual grumble. He dropped into one of the chairs facing my desk and I ignored him for a moment while I finished reading.

My office was small by most standards, with a simple desk and a couple of chairs for visitors, but I didn't need anything lavish. I kept my office in my organization's main training gym so I always knew what was going on with my fighters and their trainers. They were my bread and butter, so I split my time between the gym and corporate.

That gym was the life force of my business. My biggest fighters trained there and if anything went wrong, I needed to know immediately. My competition thought my time was better served elsewhere, but that was why the MMAC was successful and they weren't.

"Sorry to interrupt you, but I got a physical therapist coming in today for an interview," he said.

I slowly turned to face Mack, surprised by his announcement. "It's about time," I said.

"I know you've suggested it for a while. And I know the other trainers have done good having someone help with their fighters' injuries, but you know I like to work alone."

"What prompted this?" I asked.

He grumbled as his face twisted into a grimace. "My niece. She asked me to meet this *girl*. It's some friend of hers."

"Girl?" I asked, surprised a woman would be interested in working in what was thought to be the bloodiest sport today. "She could be an asset to your team."

Mack grunted as he slumped back in his chair. Mack had worked for me from the beginning. He was one of my best trainers, and one of the most stubborn, too.

"What is it about women?" he grumbled as he shook his head. "Becca's my niece, but I jump every time she needs something."

"That's because you're a good man, Mack. I know you have a soft spot in there."

"Bah, soft spot! Now I have this girl coming in," he said, sighing. "You're not going to force me to hire her, are you?"

"No, but give her a chance. I've seen some of your new fighters, and they're sloppy. They'll get injured easily and you don't want them out for too long. Give it some thought."

"Yeah, yeah, whatever," Mack grumbled as he got up to leave my office.

"What time is she coming in?"

Mack narrowed his eyes at me. "I mean no disrespect, but stay away from her. The last thing I need if I hire her is you screwing around with her head."

"You don't know what you're talking about, Mack," I said as I glared back at him. "I'm only asking because a stranger is coming into my training facility."

"Oh, sorry," he said, looking down. "2 o'clock."

I turned away from him as he shuffled into the hall. This had nothing to do with a woman coming to the gym. I personally liked to know whenever there were guests. I had been in this business long enough to know I could only trust a small handful of people.

***

It was 2 o'clock, not just the end of my workout, but time for Mack's interview to come in. After a few minutes of hitting the speed bag, I had my personal trainer cut the wraps from my hands and I walked over to the ring where Mack was watching his new fighter.

She caught my attention right away. It wasn't just having a woman in the gym, I was drawn to her. With her shoulder-length dark wavy hair, the way her shirt hugged her breasts, and her round ass, she was just my type. And after my vigorous workout strained and hardened my muscles, I couldn't help but wonder what her soft body would feel like pressed against me.

But there was something else about her. An innocence in her wide eyes that I rarely saw anymore. When she caught me looking at her, I couldn't help but smile, but when she shyly turned away, I knew I had to have her.

I caught Mack's stern expression as he met my gaze. I knew what he was thinking and he was right. There had been one too many ring girls in my past who had left this training facility in tears when they realized I wasn't as serious about them as they thought. They thought they could change me. They believed it when I said they were special. As a man, I had needs. I'd say anything to get what I wanted.

But something in me said this woman had a lot more to offer. She wasn't someone to just have fun with. While people like Mack thought I was heartless, I didn't like breaking anyone's heart. I was going to wait and introduce myself to her, but instead I turned and walked away. I had no right thinking about a woman. I had too many commitments and responsibilities to add anything serious to my plate.

As I turned towards the locker room, her voice echoed through the gym. It didn't sound like anything I expected to come out of such a sweet-looking face. I turned back to watch what was going on and saw her fist come down hard on the ring floor.

"Left hook! Throw a fucking left hook!" she yelled.

I laughed and forced myself to walk away. She was going to be harder to forget than I thought. And knowing Mack, she just cursed her way into a job.

As my personal trainer opened the door to the locker room, I couldn't stop thinking about her. Who was this curvy woman with the mouth of a sailor? All I knew was if I was left alone with her, I wouldn't be able to control myself. I had to make her mine.

Chapter Three

Cassie

I spent my first week at work avoiding Gabriel. Every time I saw him, I went in the other direction. I just couldn't face him, not after that kiss. Not when just the memory of it made my legs go weak. It made me feel ridiculous.

How does a grown woman get wobbly like that? I wanted to blame all the testosterone in the air, my nerves, anything, but I knew it was just his effect on me. There was something about Gabriel Kohl that I wasn't able to shake.

Sitting across the desk from me was the fighter I yelled at in the ring to get this job. Ryan, like the rest of the fighters in the gym, had an incredible body. I definitely couldn't complain about the eye candy.

Mack had set me up with an office off the locker room. It was private with a desk in the corner of the room and an examination table in the center. He had scheduled several fighters to meet with me every day so that I could get to know his team. Ryan was the last of them.

Ryan went on and on about his arm with his Southern drawl. He described the many injuries he had sustained over his short career and what had been done in the past to correct them. I forced myself to take some notes as I tried to focus on his words, but I was getting impatient as it got closer to three o'clock.

By my second day there, I realized Gabriel's limo arrived around three o'clock and he left shortly after. Even though I was avoiding him, I still enjoyed looking at him every chance I got.

"Well thank you, Ryan," I said. "I have an open door policy so if you ever have any questions or if that arm acts up again, you know where to find me."

Ryan smiled and nodded as he rose from the chair.

"Thanks, Miss Monroe," he said.

"Please, call me Cassie."

Ryan lifted his hand in a short wave as he walked out of my office. I got up and quickly walked around to the other side of the desk, smoothed down my shirt, and pushed my hair back behind my ear as I walked out the door. I knew it was crazy, but watching Gabriel leave was the highlight of my day.

As I rounded the corner, Ryan caught up with me.

"I was hoping to catch you out of your office, Miss Monroe, Cassie," he said as he inched closer.

"Oh? Did you have a question? Is your arm still bothering you?"

"It's fine," he said as he flexed his bicep, his drawl becoming more pronounced. "I just think you're really nice."

He touched my hair and I backed away, not realizing the corner was behind me. Ryan moved closer to me, boxing me in.

"Don't touch me," I said, slapping his hand away.

"Just give me a chance, Cassie, you'll see how nice I can be, too," he said as his hand slid down my arm.

"Leave me the fuck alone," I said as I pushed at him with all my might.

When he wouldn't budge, I tried to move as far into the corner as possible, but Ryan didn't seem to care what I said or did.

"She said to leave her the fuck alone."

Gabriel's commanding voice came from behind Ryan. Everything moved so quickly that the next thing I knew, Gabriel was holding Ryan against him. Gabriel's forearm was pressed against Ryan's neck, and Gabriel's hand was locked on the bicep of his other arm. I didn't have to work in the gym to recognize a rear naked choke.

Ryan's hands were on Gabriel's arm as he tried to get out, but Gabriel had him tight. He gasped for air as Gabriel sank the hold further. Gabriel's eyes were fierce, unlike anything I had seen before.

"Apologize," Gabriel said.

Ryan grunted, his face turning red. "Sorry, ma'am," he said.

"If I hear you do anything like that again, you're done. You'll never fight again. Do you understand?" Gabriel said, still holding him.

Ryan nodded as best as he could, his face beginning to turn purple. His hand tapped fast on Gabriel's arm. As Gabriel released him, he pushed him forward and Ryan dropped to his knees.

Gabriel glared at him for a moment, then brushed his button-down shirt with his hands. Turning to me, he held out his hand.

"Come with me," he said.

I took his hand and he pulled me out of the corner and down the hall towards the front of the gym.

"Thank you," I whispered, too stunned to speak up.

"Are you okay?"

"Yes, I'm fine. He just surprised me."

"When I didn't see you at the front of the gym, I had to find you," he said.

"You saw me? I didn't know you noticed."

"I always notice you," he said as he looked at his watch. "I'm sorry, I have to get going. Are you sure you're okay?"

I nodded, and he kissed my forehead before walking out of the gym and getting into the limo. From behind me, I heard someone clear his throat. I turned around to find Ryan with his head hanging down and his hands clasped together as if he was praying.

"I'm sorry, Miss Monroe," he said. "I didn't realize you were taken."

"Taken? I'm not...never mind. It's okay, Ryan, but even so, I told you to leave me alone."

"You said to leave you the fuck alone," he said with a smile. "I promise it'll never happen again."

I looked out the window and saw the limo had already pulled away. I had tomorrow at three o'clock to look forward to.

***

The next day, I was updating the records I had on each fighter when I looked up and saw it was just after three.

Dammit! I lost track of time!

I rushed out of my office and turned down the hall that led to the front of the building. At the other end of the hall, Gabriel stood and looked at his watch, then raised his eyebrows at me.

"You're late," he said.

"I thought I had missed you."

"I was waiting for you. After yesterday, I wanted to make sure nothing else happened to you."

He stepped closer, cupped my face with his large hand, then slowly pushed my hair back over my ear. I tilted my face towards him, hoping for a kiss, but instead he turned towards the front windows where his driver was standing by his limo.

"I have to go," he said. He pulled a small gift-wrapped box out of the black wool coat he was wearing and handed it to me. "Just a glimpse of you is enough for me right now, but I want more. Don't be late again."

"What is this? I can't--"

His lips pressed against mine, silencing me.

"It's yours," he said.

Before I could say anything else, he left. I held the box in my hands as I watched him stride through the front door towards the limo.

Turn around, Gabriel. Please turn around. Give me a sign that says I'm not crazy for liking you.

With the door opened, he turned and looked back towards the gym, then pointed towards me and mouthed the words 'open it'. I looked down at the box and shook my head. *What could it be?*

Turning back towards the window, I saw his limo was gone.

I took the box to my office and locked the door as I entered. I wanted to keep the present private, to myself. Whatever it was, I didn't want to share it with anyone who might walk past.

Sitting down, I pulled the ribbon off and ripped into the thick fancy gift wrapping, revealing a white box with the word *'Cartier'* written in gold in the center. Inside the white box was a small card on top of a cushioned dark red box with small gold designs around the edge. I opened the card.

Promise never to be late again.

I smiled and laughed to myself as I lifted the lid of the red box. As I looked inside, I gasped. It was beautiful! Wrapped around a small ivory pillow in the middle of the box was a diamond Cartier watch.

The face was oval with black Roman numerals and blue hands. Diamonds surrounded the oval and lined the thin band. I slipped it onto my wrist and watched it sparkle.

While I loved it, I couldn't help but think it was too much. He barely knew me, and I couldn't even imagine what something like that cost.

Probably more than I could imagine.

I had to give it back. I took the watch off and as I slipped it back onto the pillow in the box, the watch slipped and flipped over. The back was engraved.

You can't say no, it's yours.
--Gabriel

"Well, twist my arm," I said, taking the watch out of the box again.

There was no saying no to Gabriel. I put the watch back on my wrist and smiled, feeling closer to him. I'd have to convince him to take the watch back another time. No matter what he said, it was just too much.

***

Days had passed and I was still floating in my own world. I couldn't stop thinking about how Gabriel had rescued me from Ryan and later gave me the watch. He was becoming an addiction, and I couldn't allow myself to think of him like that. I had to remember I had a job, my dream job, and I didn't want to do anything to mess that up. But I also couldn't help myself.

It was nearly three o'clock, so I fixed my hair and snuck a quick peek in the mirror. Gabriel and I had been spending a few minutes together before he left each day. As I walked out, I found him leaning against the wall on the other side of my doorway with a big grin on his face.

"I could set a watch by you," he said.

"I don't know what you're talking about. Now if you don't mind, I'm meeting someone in a few minutes."

I tried to keep a straight face as I tapped my watch. But as I looked at the watch, my stomach sank. It took no time for me to feel comfortable wearing it. Not only did I forget I was going to give it back to him, but I forgot to thank him for it, too.

"Is something wrong?" he asked, his brow wrinkling.

"I can't take this," I said, removing the watch. "It's beautiful, too beautiful really. Thank you...but I can't accept this." I looked at the watch for a moment and then placed it in his hand.

"I got this for you," he said softly, holding his hand out to me. "It's yours."

"No, it's too much, Gabriel. I barely know you and you're my boss. I can't even imagine what it cost."

"The cost doesn't matter. I saw it and thought you would like it." He took my hand and held it. "Do you like it?"

I hated to admit that I did, but as I looked into his eyes, I knew I couldn't lie. As I nodded, he slipped the watch back onto my wrist.

"All that matters is that you like it," he said.

I smiled up at him, but something still didn't feel right. Mack's voice echoed from down the hall as he yelled at a fighter. As I looked up at Gabriel, his hand still holding mine, I couldn't get it out of my mind that he was my boss.

"Thank you, but--"

"But nothing," he said, interrupting me. "Like it says on the back, it's yours." He looked towards the windows at the front of the gym, then back at me. His limo was waiting. "I've had enough of this, Cassie. I want to get to know you better, and a few minutes a day isn't cutting it."

"No, a few minutes is perfect." I looked away, unable to lie to his face. "I'm just busy and I have a lot to learn. You know how it is at a new job."

"Then join me for dinner tonight. We can get to know each other better without a time limit. And if you have a lot to learn, I bet there's a lot I can teach you," he said with a mischievous look.

I wanted to say yes. I wanted to run out the door and jump into his limo that very second and have him whisk me away, but I wanted the job more. I had waited too long and tried too hard to get a job like this. No matter how attracted I was to him, I wasn't going to risk losing my job.

I also knew from experience that men didn't always hang around. As Mack's voice echoed back down the hall, I remembered what he said about Gabriel after my interview, about how I shouldn't expect Gabriel to want more than just fun. He was a player, and I didn't want to play games. Especially not with him.

"No, no. I can't join you for dinner. I know I work for Mack, but you're the owner, so that makes you my boss. I need this job and I'm not going to do anything to fuck it up."

His eyes narrowed and he licked his lips slowly as he looked at me. I wondered what he was thinking, but I was willing to bet he didn't get rejected very often.

"We'll talk about this another time," he said as he looked at his watch before turning and walking away.

Chapter Four

Cassie

Sitting at my desk, I crossed out another day on my desk calendar, tracing the X over and over with the pen, watching the X darken. I couldn't get Gabriel out of my mind. It had been days since Gabriel had been in the gym and I couldn't help but think it was my fault.

A knock on my office door made me jump to attention. Hoping to see Gabriel standing in the doorway, I was disappointed to see Jake. Jake was a heavyweight with thick muscles, long arms, and a shock of platinum spiked hair. He was wearing a pair of loose fitting fleece pants and a tight black t-shirt.

"Is it a good time?" he asked, smiling shyly.

"Of course, come in," I said, standing.

As Jake entered the room, I noticed a slight limp. I pulled out a padded wooden chair and patted the back.

"Sit," I said. "I don't want you to deal with sitting on the table right now."

"Is it that obvious?" he whispered. "Can you close the door?"

His eyes darted towards the door. I walked to the door and closed it. For the first time, I realized how my office being off the locker rooms was both a blessing and a curse. My location made it easy for the fighters to come in and find me, but for anyone paying attention, it made it easy to know who was injured.

"What happened?" I asked.

"I don't know," Jake said, shaking his head. "I think my foot landed wrong while I was running." He pulled up his pants leg to his knee and pointed under his kneecap. "The pain is here. Last time it felt like this, I tore my meniscus. You've gotta help me."

His eyes widened as they pleaded with me. I turned away from him and crossed my arms in front of me. I needed to think, and looking at his sad face wasn't going to help. I knew Mack had a lot of faith in Jake and this fight was something that could move Jake up in the ranks. Sighing, I put on a pair of exam gloves and kneeled in front of him.

"Let me know if it hurts," I said.

I touched his kneecap, then pressed gently under and to the sides of his knee. His leg trembled and jerked from my touch. He didn't say anything, but he didn't have to, I knew he was in pain. Lifting his leg, I straightened it at the knee and heard a click. I was sure he was right about his meniscus.

"Have you been to the doctor? You should get an MRI to make sure it's not something else," I said.

"No, I can't go. No one can know I'm injured. I have a fight next week, I can't pull out of it."

"You can't fight like this. They're going to see you limp and kick that knee until you collapse. It's what I would do," I said with a grin.

"I'm a wrestler. I'll take him down at the bell and then ground and pound him. That's my speciality," he said.

"And when you get him on the ground and your knee hits the mat, you're going to feel it right here," I said, touching his knee and making him groan in pain.

"That's why I'm here. Mack said I could trust you. You've gotta help me."

Standing up, I tossed the exam gloves into the trash. I knew he could fight with a torn meniscus, but he didn't need to just fight, he needed to win. I opened my supply cabinet and pulled out an extra large compression brace for his knee and took it out of its packaging.

"You need to lay off on the training," I said as I knelt in front of him again. "You don't want this getting worse, and you don't want it getting out that you're limping. When you're in the gym, you have to wear this." I held up the brace. "It should help prevent any additional swelling and give you a little support."

He took the brace, slipped off his sandal, and pulled the brace up his thick leg and moved it in place.

"How's that feel?" I asked.

"Good. Better than the last one," he said, smiling.

"Do you have crutches at home from last time?"

"Yeah, I've been using them to get around."

"Keep doing that, but try to rest. Ice your knee and keep it elevated. When you're not icing, wear the brace."

"Thanks," he said as he stood.

He began walking to the door and while his limp wasn't as pronounced, I could still see it.

"Come on, Jake," I said. "There's only so much I can do. After the fight, you have to promise you'll see the doctor. He needs to make sure it's not anything else."

"I promise, after the fight. Right now I don't need anyone to know I'm injured though."

"Then stop limping!"

His brows shot up. "I thought I was doing better."

"Yes, you are, but I can still see you're favoring that side."

"I don't know what to do," he said, shaking his head.

I patted Jake on the back as I let out a deep breath. I worked with some of the strongest and toughest men in the world. They could take punches, kicks, sometimes even break bones in the cage and not complain. But out of the cage, when that adrenaline wasn't fueling them, they crumbled from the slightest thing. I only had one option.

"Jake, you're a fighter," I said. "Do you want to win? Or do you want to get your ass kicked?"

"I want to win," he said quietly.

"No, you don't want to just win, you want to fucking win, right?"

He grinned, and a fire lit in his eyes.

"That's right," he said, his voice growing more confident. "I'm going to take him down and fucking win. I'm not going to let him stand in the way of that belt. I win and it's one step closer."

"Exactly. So man up and walk without a limp. Suck it up and just do it. All you have to do is get from point A to point B. Then once you're in the octagon, kick his ass."

Jake took a deep breath and stepped closer to the door, but this time I didn't see a limp.

"I will. Thanks, Cassie! Mack was right, he said you would help me."

Smiling, I watched Jake leave the office then picked up the plastic wrapper that held the brace. Each time a fighter came to me and I was able to help him, it was like a pat on the back. I loved this job more than I ever thought I would.

I put the wrapper into the trash as Mack entered my office and closed the door. His watery eyes danced as a small smile spread across his face.

"I just passed Jake," he said. "Whatever you did worked. He's going to win that fight."

Mack pulled the chair back at an angle in front of my desk and sat down. Leaning back, he put his feet up on the chair in front of him.

Shrugging, I sat in my seat and leaned forward to rest my elbows on the desk.

"I really didn't do anything," I said. "Just gave him a compression wrap and told him how to take care of his knee until he gets it checked out."

"Bah, I know you. You said something to him. I'm sure you gave him a brace, but you and I both know that's not what helped him."

"What can I say? I took a page out of your book and told him to man up."

Mack threw his head back and laughed. "I wish I had been here for that. That's what I like about you, Cassie, you're not afraid to push these guys around when you need to. I'm glad you're here. I wasn't sure I needed a physical therapist on my team, but I can't imagine doing this without you now."

"Aww, Mack. Are you getting soft on me?" I teased.

"You ever tell anyone and I'll deny it to my deathbed," he grunted.

"Hey, you know I've been wanting to ask you something. I saw there's a fight in a couple of months in Vegas, should I plan to go to that?"

"You don't have to. As you know, normally we have our fights here in the coliseum. Every so often Gabriel schedules one elsewhere, but he never goes. I'd love to have you there of course, and I know the fighters would too. It hasn't been long, but you've become one of the family. But I suspect Gabriel will want you around here."

"What makes you think that?"

"Ha! I may be old, Cassie, but I'm not blind," Mack said with a laugh. "I've seen how he looks at you and how you meet before he leaves."

"Oh, well, I don't know what you're talking about," I muttered as I looked down at my desk and fumbled with a pencil.

Mack swiped the pencil out of my hand and leaned back in his chair. He bounced the eraser tip on the desk as he shook his head at me.

"I'm also not stupid," he said, grinning.

"Okay, I know you said to stay away from the suit but..." I said as I shrugged.

Mack chuckled and set the pencil down. He slid his fingers into his silver hair and rubbed the side of his head.

"I don't say this often, but sometimes I'm wrong," he said. "I know deep down he's a good man, even if he is a suit. I meant it when I said to stay away from him, but now I don't know."

"What do you mean?" I asked.

Mack pursed his lips and breathed out slowly. He tilted his head as he looked at me and stroked the white stubble on his chin. I was ready to jump across the desk and throttle him for torturing me.

Dammit, tell me already! I thought.

"I don't know. Maybe he's different, maybe he's not," he said with a shrug. "By now he'd be on to someone else."

"There's been a lot of girls before?"

I really didn't want to know the answer, but I had to ask. I braced myself as Mack squinted his eyes and rubbed his chin.

"Not so much recently, but a tiger can't change his stripes. Remember that," he grumbled.

"I'm telling you now I don't want you blubbering to me about him. I warned ya about him. Just because I haven't seen it in a while doesn't mean it's not happening. Just be careful, I guess is all I'm sayin'."

"I know, I know. And you said you thought there was someone."

"That's right," he said, standing. "He might be smitten with you right now, but I can tell when a man has it bad for someone and I'm sure Gabriel does. I have no place in telling you what to do, but be careful with that one. He could be playing games with you."

In the short time that I had been there, Mack had become something of a father figure to me. I smiled as I watched him walk out the office, knowing he had my best interest at heart. It didn't matter how much he warned me about Gabriel though, I couldn't get him out of my mind.

***

It was just my luck the clouds opened up and it started to rain as I reached the bus stop. I tried to squeeze in under the crowded canopy, but there wasn't enough room. Leaning towards the street, I looked around, hoping the bus would be early.

The wind was beginning to kick up and the rain poured sideways. As I brushed my hair out of my face, a black limo pulled up in front of the bus stop. The waiting crowd ignored the limo, but I couldn't take my eyes off it. I kept thinking about Gabriel and hoping it was him.

The window lowered and Gabriel leaned forward into view, his hair falling forward onto his forehead. He was wearing a dark suit now instead of the casual clothing I normally saw him in. His blue eyes moved up and down my body as a smile spread across his lips.

"Get in," he said, opening the door with a smile.

I stepped forward, ready to do anything he said, but then stopped myself. What was I thinking? I had to stop thinking of Gabriel as this sexy man I wanted to see naked and remember he was my boss.

"No, thank you" I said, stepping back towards the bus stop. "I don't mind waiting."

"It wasn't a question, Cassie. I said get in."

He pushed the door further open and without a second thought, I slipped into the back of the limo. I pushed back my wet hair from my face and tried to look like I had been in a limo a million times before.

I wiped the rain from my eyes, very aware of him staring at me. Of all the times for him to see me, it had to be now that I looked like a drowned rat. Gabriel leaned down, reached into a gym bag that was near his feet, and pulled out a white gym towel and handed it to me.

"Here, take this. Don't worry, it's clean," he said.

I took the towel and patted my face, trying to make myself look like not as much of a mess. I felt Gabriel's eyes on me and fidgeted in my seat.

Why was he staring? Was my hair sticking straight up? I reached up and tried smoothing my hair down. *Maybe there was something on my face.* I turned towards the window and tried to catch my reflection when Gabriel's hand pulled mine from my face. I turned towards him and my eyes immediately locked on his.

"Relax," he said. "The rain made you even more beautiful."

"Thank you," I whispered, unsure what else to say.

A flush crept up my neck and I looked down then back out the window, hoping he didn't see the effect he had on me. With his looks, I couldn't help but think he had this effect on most women and he knew exactly what he was doing.

"Where's your car?" he asked.

"I don't have one," I said.

I wanted to tell him why, but I bit my tongue to stop myself. As I looked at his angled jaw and intense eyes, I wanted to tell him everything. It wasn't like me at all.

"As my employee, you're going to need a car in order to get around. I can arrange something for you."

"No. If I need a car, I'll get one myself," I said. "I just need a little time."

He nodded as his eyes narrowed. I could see his brain working and wondered what he was thinking.

"Where are you headed?"

"Home," I said, then realized what he meant. "But you don't need to take me. I can wait for the bus."

"No. I won't have you waiting for the bus, especially not in this rain," he said. He rolled down the divider between us and the driver. "Tell Stan where to take you."

I looked towards the front of the limo and noticed the driver looking back at me in his rearview mirror. He had kind brown eyes and curly grey hair. I racked my brain, trying to think about where I could tell him to take me. I didn't want them to see where I lived.

If it were anyone else, I wouldn't have cared. I was proud of having my own place, even if it was just a room. I loved the old, run-down neighborhood, but someone as rich as Gabriel would never understand. I looked at the driver, then back at Gabriel, then down at the floor. *Shit!* I was drawing blanks. I didn't have a choice.

"356 Highland Boulevard," I said.

"South End?" Stan asked.

"Yes," I whispered.

The divider rose between the driver and Gabriel and I, leaving us alone again. Gabriel took the towel from my hands and slowly started to towel dry my hair.

"You'll catch your death out there," he said. "I'm glad I drove past. I would have been here sooner but I had to take care of some things first."

I didn't know what to say. He finished drying my hair then folded the towel and placed it neatly back into his gym bag. I forced myself to look out the window to stop staring at him.

As I looked outside, I watched as the green grass disappeared and the tall buildings were replaced with old battered houses and buildings. Even the street went from smooth pavement to bumpy, pothole-ridden roads. The neighborhood looked worse than it did this morning and I knew it was because I was seeing it through Gabriel's eyes.

I would have happily taken the bus just to avoid Gabriel seeing all of this, but none of it seemed to faze him. He leaned towards me and I felt his breath hot against my ear.

"I spent a lot of time in that old building on the corner with the mural," he said.

Darting my eyes to the building, I saw a mural of a fighter hitting a speed bag. I never noticed it before. As the limo drove past, I saw the word 'Gym' etched into the stone above the door. I wanted to ask him why he had slummed it down here, but even though my eyes were focused outside, I knew Gabriel's eyes were focused on me.

He leaned in closer and swept my hair back from my neck. I thought time stood still as I waited for his lips to brush against my skin. When they did, it sent a shiver through my body and it wiped everything from my mind.

Stan turned at the corner of Highland Boulevard, drove past the bus stop, and slowed down. The divider lowered between us and in the rearview mirror, I saw his brown eyes looking back at me again as he waited for instructions.

"It's up a little further on the right," I said. "But you can leave me here, I can walk."

"You're not walking," Gabriel said. "I want to make sure you get home okay. This is a rough neighborhood."

"No, you don't need to do that. I walk around here all the time. I'm sure you wouldn't walk Mack up to his front door."

"I also wouldn't give Mack a ride home. But you're not Mack," he said. "You're much prettier."

The limo pulled up in front of the painted brick building Becca and I lived in. Strips of dark red paint hung from the brick, revealing its age and neglect. I opened the car door as the driver stepped out, and as I got out of the car, Gabriel stepped out behind me.

"What are you doing?" I asked, spinning around to face him.

"I'm making sure you get home okay, remember?"

"No, just stop," I said. "This is way too much."

It was bad enough he was there in front of my building. I didn't want him to see the inside of the apartment. It wasn't even really my apartment, it was Becca's apartment. I rented a room.

"You don't have a choice," he said. "Open the door."

His eyes told me he meant every word. We walked to the door and I pulled my keys out of my bag. I hesitated before unlocking it and saw his eyebrow rise. He pushed open the heavy front door and we entered the stark hall with two apartment doors. Gabriel cocked his brow at me.

"Which way?" he asked.

I moved to our apartment door and slowly started unlocking the locks. I kept hoping he'd get tired and leave, but I wasn't that lucky. Once the door was open, he put his hand on the small of my back and entered the apartment with me.

The place was so tiny that he crossed the living room and kitchen with three long strides. He didn't seem to notice the shabby, wheat-colored couch or the folding chairs around the card table Becca and I ate at. When his hand touched the stair rail, my heart leapt into my throat.

"No," I said. "Don't go up there."

"Why not? Are you hiding something?" he said with a grin before he started climbing the steps.

"No, but stop! What are you doing? You shouldn't even be here," I said as I rushed behind him. "Fuck! Why won't you listen?"

I grabbed his arm to stop him as he reached the top of the steps. As we stood on the small landing, he looked at the three doors then moved to open Becca's door.

"Gabriel, no!"

He turned back towards me, and his eyes studied my face as his face softened.

"Which one is yours?" he asked.

Tilting my head towards the accordion door, I hoped he wouldn't slide the door open, but by now I knew better. Gabriel was going to do whatever he wanted. He took a small step so he was standing in front of my bedroom door and put his hand on the thick piece of plastic that controlled the door.

His face went blank and then his head lowered, but he didn't open the door. Slowly, he turned towards me.

"You have to move," he said quietly. "You deserve better than this."

"Yeah, I'll get right on that," I said, laughing. "I know, I can move to a fancy neighborhood. Maybe you'll like that better."

"This isn't about me. Look at this place, Cassie. This isn't a bedroom. You have no privacy. I could knock this piece of shit door down if I tapped it hard enough."

"Well, what am I supposed to do? This was all I could afford," I said, crossing my arms in front of me as my temper rose. "Do you want to know why I don't have a car? Because I had to sell it to pay for this place. Life isn't that easy for us normal people. Not everyone can be a billionaire, you know."

I couldn't look at him anymore. If I had to stand there for another minute, knowing he felt sorry for me, I might punch him. I didn't care if he went into my bedroom. I didn't care that he probably couldn't fit between the furniture to enter the room. I just wanted him gone.

As I went downstairs, I heard the vinyl door slide open. The floor creaked underneath him. *I can't believe him!* I fought every urge of mine to storm back upstairs and give him more hell when I heard the furniture in my room sliding along the floor. *What is he doing?*

I raced back upstairs and found Gabriel had pushed my dresser so that there was more space. His eyes looked dark and his jaw was set.

"You can stay here one more night if you need to, but you have to move," he said. "I have an apartment near the gym you can move into. It's close enough that you can walk to work."

"What are you saying? I'm not moving in with you."

He laughed and walked past me out of the room.

"It's the weekend. I'll have Stan arrange for movers in the morning," he said as he started to go down the stairs.

"I'm not moving," I said, trying to catch up to him as he reached the first floor.

"I'll repeat what I said earlier – you don't have a choice. Let me put it this way. If you want to continue working for me, you're going to live where I say."

I didn't know what to say. As I stood there, dumbfounded, unsure what had just happened. Gabriel stopped by the door and turned around. His face softened and a smile threatened on his lips before he strode out of our apartment and stepped outside the main door where his limo was still waiting. He slipped inside and closed the door behind him.

Standing in the doorway, I watched his limo pull away. I couldn't see him behind the dark windows, but I knew he was looking at me. I still wanted to fight him. I wanted to say I was my own person and I would pay my own way, but everything happened so fast I couldn't get the words out. I'd have to deal with it tomorrow. I didn't care what he said, I was not moving into his apartment.

Chapter Five

Gabriel

Seeing where Cassie lived brought back too many memories, and none of them were good. I thought I was past that, that I never had to deal with going to the South End again, but there I was and it all came rushing back.

Ten Years Ago

As I walked up the block, the streetlight came on, lighting up the fighter mural on the side of the gym. That image meant the world to me. I had been fighting all my life, it only made sense that I would become a fighter, too.

Over the past couple of years, the gym's popularity had grown. It went from just being a home for boxers to offering training in Brazilian jiu-jitsu and more. MMA was growing so a few friends of mine pooled their money together, bought the old neighborhood gym, and offered MMA training.

I wasn't interested in all that responsibility though. Fighting was it for me. It gave me an outlet to release all my anger. Knocking a guy out, or better yet, feeling him tap out during a submission was what kept me going. Well, that and pussy.

As I entered the gym, one of the guys pointed to my mouth. I nodded and pulled out a towel from my bag and wiped the lipstick from my mouth. Penny liked to leave her mark on me. I was lucky it was just lipstick. She left another mark somewhere else, but none of the fighters would be seeing that.

While I made my way to the lockers, my trainer Vince caught up with me. He was a small man with a shaved head and was built like a tank.

"You're late, Kohl," Vince said. "And not only that, but how many times have I told you, no personal calls."

"Who was it this time?" I asked as I put my bag into a locker.

"I don't know, she could barely speak. She was slurring really bad."

"Dakota," I said, pulling my bag back out of the locker. "Did she say where she is?"

"Yeah, Highland Boulevard. 972 I think. Wait, you're not leaving, are you?"

"She needs me," I said as I left the gym.

Dakota had been my girl since we were kids. We did everything together, even experimented with drugs. But while I needed to stay clean to be a fighter, Dakota let the drugs take hold.

As I sprinted to Highland Boulevard, I cursed everything. I was familiar with the address she gave Vince, I'd pulled her out of there several times before. 972 Highland Boulevard was a drug den.

Several potheads were hanging out on the front stoop when I got there. One of them, a scraggily guy with bleached dreadlocks, looked familiar. I yanked him up from his seat and pressed him against the wall of the building.

"Where is she?" I demanded.

"Oh hey man, I remember you. Gabriel, right? Like the angel," he said as he drifted off.

"Where's Dakota?" I asked, shaking him.

"Oh yeah, Dakota. Probably on the second floor with the other dopers."

I dropped him and pushed past several people to get into the house. I took the steps two at a time as they groaned and creaked under my weight. The long hallway had several open doors, but I didn't know which one Dakota could be in.

"Dakota!" I called out, hoping she hadn't passed out or worse.

"In here," she said.

Following her voice, I entered a room at the end of the hall. It was like many others I had been in before to rescue her from. The rooms were either dumps with dirty mattresses strewn around or they were partitioned off into makeshift rooms with vinyl folding doors.

"Just keep following my voice, Gabe," she said.

Her voice led me to a closed brown vinyl accordion door. I slid it open and found her lying on a ratty mattress. The smell of vomit was in the air. Dakota's long dark hair was matted and wet from sweat, and she looked thinner than I remembered.

"It's okay, Dakota," I said. "I'm here. I'm going to take you home."

"This is home," she said with a laugh, her voice hoarse. "I've spent more time in here or in places like it over the years than I have in my own apartment."

My brow wrinkled, hearing her speak. It was the clearest I had heard her in a long time. I looked at her green eyes and was surprised to find them clear.

"Are you clean?" I asked.

She nodded slowly. "Been clean for two weeks now."

"Then why are you here?"

"Because I didn't know where else to go," she said. "I had to get clean. I'm pregnant. This baby needs a fighting chance."

"Pregnant," I said as I tried to remember the last time Dakota and I were together.

"Relax, it's not yours," she said.

"You have to get out of here. This isn't the place for a pregnant woman. You know I love you, Dakota, I always have. Let me help."

I picked her up, cradling her in my arms and carrying her down the stairs and outside. The cool night air made her shiver.

"You're the best thing that ever happened to me, Gabriel. I'd probably be dead by now if it wasn't for you."

"I'm taking you home. To my home," I said as I walked up the street with her in my arms. "Marry me, Dakota."

"You're fucking crazy," she said as she laughed.

"Marry me and I'll take care of you for the rest of your life."

Present Day

I couldn't let Cassie stay in that shithole knowing the kind of things that happened in places like that. It wasn't safe, and I'd be damned if I was going to sit by and let something happen to her. I cared too much about her and I knew the things that went on in that neighborhood. She deserved better.

Chapter Six

Cassie

"That arrogant ass," I grumbled.

I continued flipping through the TV channels, looking for a distraction, but nothing caught my eye. I pulled my feet underneath me on the couch and stewed as I thought about Gabriel. He put me in such a bad mood, I couldn't think about anything else but what he said.

You don't have a choice.

Each time his words repeated in my head, I came up with something good to say back to him. Why didn't this happen earlier when he was here? Instead I got lost in his blue eyes again. Those dark blue eyes...

Dammit! Not again!

Behind me, I heard Becca unlocking the series of locks on our door as she came home.

Becca worked two jobs. During the day, she worked at a satellite office for the Canyon Cove Housing Authority a few blocks from the apartment, and then in the evenings she waitressed at a hip restaurant downtown. She stepped inside and dropped her messenger bag on the cushion next to me, then turned on the lights.

"You're sitting in the dark again?" she asked.

"You know how expensive electricity is. And I'm not in the dark, the TV is on."

She shook her head, laughing, as she grabbed a glass, filled it with water, and took a sip.

"I'm sure your mother would have something to say about that," she said.

"Yeah, well my mother has plenty to say about a lot of things," I said, laughing. "How long are you home?"

"I've got to leave in twenty minutes. Why? Everything okay?"

"Everything's fine," I said with a shrug. "Just wanted to talk."

"I know that tone, Cassie. You sure you're alright?"

"Yes, don't worry about me. Go get ready for work. It can wait until you get home from the restaurant tonight."

"I don't know. Aren't those your work clothes? You always change as soon as you get home. Something's going on," she said.

Becca looked at me over her glass as she took a quick gulp. She was torn, but the last thing I wanted was for her to be late for work. I gave her a big smile and waved my hands, motioning for her to go upstairs.

"Really, I'm fine," I said. "Don't worry about me. Go get ready for work."

"Okay, I'll go," she said. "What about your cousin? Didn't you say you have a cousin in Canyon Cove? Have you called her yet?"

"No, I haven't. My mom emailed me her number, but I feel a little weird reaching out to her after all this time."

"You're being silly, Cassie. Just call her. You said you were close once, that never changes. Call her."

Becca ran up the stairs and the sound of the shower came on. I didn't mind being alone, but Gabriel had me so frustrated, I needed someone to vent to. But how could I vent to someone I hadn't seen in over a decade?

Picking up my phone, I opened up the email from my mother and looked at Ashley's number. It had been so long, I felt weird reaching out to her. At the bottom of the email, my mother had attached a picture of Ashley and I together when we were teens.

In the photo, I was wearing a pink shirt and was smiling directly at the camera. Ashley was sticking her tongue out at me as her hands reached for my neck. I laughed, remembering that day and how much she and I shared together. It was one of the last times I saw her. She moved away a few weeks later.

I missed her. It had been years since I really thought about her, but seeing that picture reminded me of how close we really were. Without hesitation, I tapped on the phone number and listened as Ashley's phone rang.

"Hello?" Ashley said, answering.

"Ashley! I can't believe you sound exactly the same!" I said, laughing.

"Wait, this can't be! Cassie? Is it really you?"

"Yes! I'm so sorry, I was so surprised to hear your voice that I didn't say who I was."

"You didn't need to, you sound exactly the same too. How long has it been?"

"I don't know, maybe ten years. Maybe longer. My mom gave me your number. She spoke to your dad and said you're in Canyon Cove."

"Yes, I've been here a couple of years now. What about you? Last I heard, you and your mom had moved to the middle of nowhere."

"We did, we moved to Crosswicks years ago, but I had to get out of there. I'm in Canyon Cove now."

"Get out! Then you have to meet us," she said. "I'm out with a few friends right now for dinner. Do you know where Mirabella's Café in the Town Center is?"

"Of course, that's not far from where I work," I said.

"Then come meet us and we can catch up in person. I can't wait to see you."

As I hung up the phone, Becca came back downstairs in her t-shirt and jeans, obviously ready for work.

"Hey, I just got off with my cousin. I know it's out of the way, but could you drop me off at Mirabella's Café?" I asked.

"No problem. I'm glad you're meeting her. I think some fresh air will do you good. But when I get home you'll have to tell me everything that happened."

"I promise, but not until then. If I start talking about it now, I'll go crazy again," I said laughing.

"It's about your boss, isn't it?"

"You have no idea," I said, rolling my eyes.

I breathed in the chilly night air as we stepped outside and walked to Becca's red pickup truck. As Becca drove towards downtown, I tried to push Gabriel out of my mind. Tonight was about catching up with family, not about Gabriel, his lips, that body, or those blue eyes.

***

The lights from Mirabella's Café glowed through the tall windows of the restaurant. Mirabella's was one of those places I had heard a lot about, but hadn't had a chance to visit. They served a little bit of everything, but everyone raved about their pastries and desserts.

It was located in a small strip mall just a few blocks from the gym, near the bus stop. Becca pulled up in front of the restaurant and I jumped out of the car so she could speed off to work.

Walking towards the entrance slowly, I scanned the inside of Mirabella's looking for Ashley's familiar face, but didn't see her. The restaurant had dark-green metal ceiling tiles and rust-colored walls. Clusters of antique frames hung on the walls, giving the restaurant a relaxed vibe.

As I pulled open the door, Ashley popped up from her seat at a round table in the center of the restaurant and waved me over. She looked just like I remembered her with dark wavy hair and almond shaped eyes.

"I can't believe you're here," Ashley said as she hugged me tight. "You have to come over and meet Xander and Jacob sometime. I hate leaving them, but the girls practically drag me out of the house to meet them every so often."

"Hey, I understand you've got a hot husband and beautiful baby, but you need some girl time," one of her friends said, laughing.

"Cassie, that's Jackie, we went to school together," Ashley said.

Jackie was beautiful with brown hair and a creamy complexion. She pulled a chair over from a nearby table and put it between her and Ashley.

"Come sit here, Cassie," Jackie said, patting the seat. "I want to hear about the man who gave you that watch."

"Oh? Let me see," Ashley said. "You didn't tell me there was a man."

I laughed as I sat down and Jackie pulled the sleeve of my sweater back further, then nodded approvingly.

"Who said there's a man?" I said.

"No one buys themselves a watch like this," Jackie said.

"She's right, Cassie. That reminds me of something Xander would pick out," Ashley said.

Next to Ashley, an attractive woman with grey streaked blonde hair let out a low whistle. "That there is definitely a billionaire gift," she said with a Southern drawl.

"Cassie, this is Tara, and if she says it's billionaire approved, then you're holding out on us," Ashley teased.

"Okay, okay, you're right," I said, laughing. "It was a gift from a man, a wealthy one. I'll say that much."

"Deborah, you're working at that fancy department store, right? What do you think this goes for there?" Tara said to the woman next to her.

Deborah had black chin-length hair that swung forward as she took a better look at the watch. She shook her head and smiled at me.

"All I know is it says Cartier," she said, smiling. "Now if you don't mind, I'm sure Jackie and I would both like to know how you met Mr. Cartier."

"You and Jackie? What about me?" Tara said.

"You have Mason. You don't need another boyfriend," Deborah said.

"Ha! Yeah, Mason," Tara said. "He's ancient history. There's too much that happened in the past for us to move forward. Besides, you're one to talk. What about Mr. Sexy?"

"I don't even know Mr. Sexy's name," Deborah said with a wistful sigh. "Hopefully that'll change very soon."

"Right, which leaves me as the only one without any prospects here," Jackie said. "I've said it before, I'll say it again. Where's my billionaire?"

Everyone laughed, but then the last woman at the table, seated between Jackie and Deborah, leaned forward and cleared her throat. She had long, curly red hair and when she leaned back, I noticed a very visible baby bump.

"Now Jackie, you know I tried," she said. "I thought you and my brother-in-law Brent would be perfect together, but you didn't even give him a chance."

"Oh Samantha, not him again," Jackie said. "I told you, he's just not my type."

"You didn't even give him a chance," Samantha repeated.

Jackie sighed. "I just know, okay?" Jackie said before turning back to me. "Besides, this isn't about that, this is about Cassie and her Cartier watch. How did you meet him?"

"I think I'd like to hear more about everyone else. You're all much more interesting than I am," I said.

"Uh-oh," Ashley said. "I know that voice. She's hiding something from us."

"Spill it, Cassie! Inquiring minds need to know," Tara said, smirking.

"He's my boss," I said as I looked around the table, unsure what to expect. "But I don't know what's going on to be honest. This job is really important to me and I'm afraid I'm going to fuck things up."

Ashley put her arm around my shoulders and leaned in to whisper.

"Come with me to the ladies room," she said.

We excused ourselves and Ashley led me out to the back door of the restaurant. She wrapped her arms around herself briefly before quickly giving me a hug. It felt like old times.

"I thought it was better if we were outside. I didn't want anyone to hear me," she said.

"Is everything okay?"

"Absolutely! It's just what you said about your boss really hit home with me."

"Well, I'm already pretty uncomfortable with it, but earlier Gabriel drove me home and demanded I move into his apartment. There's just no way I'm doing that," I said.

"Hold on, Cassie. I know this might sound crazy, and I'm sure plenty of people would argue with me about this, but maybe you should hear him out."

"Why? Because he's a billionaire?" I said as I rolled my eyes. "I could care less about that."

"His being a billionaire is exactly why you should hear him out. I know you, Cassie. If all he was to you was your boss, you would have told him to go to hell by now. You didn't. And you accepted that watch from him. You like him, don't you?"

"Yes, but what does that have to do with his being a billionaire?"

Ashley shrugged. "They're different. I worked for Xander when we first got together and trust me, it was hard on me too. I didn't want to have a relationship with my boss. But he also had his own issues he needed to deal with. I took a lot of leaps of faith for him and I've never regretted a second of it. My dad used to tell me to trust my gut, and it was from doing that that I met the love of my life. I think maybe you need to trust your gut too."

I shook my head just to disagree even though I had a feeling she was right.

"What's the worst thing that can happen if you move into his apartment?"

"What if things don't work out? Then I'll lose my job and have no place to live on top of that. Mack said Gabriel liked playing games, what if that's all he's doing with me?" I asked.

"What's your gut say?"

"My gut is an idiot, Ashley. My gut is saying to just go along for the ride. I want him to be more than my boss, but my head--"

"Don't listen to your head. Sometimes we need to throw caution to the wind and just go with it. Listen, Cassie. I know how you are. I know you're going to fight him and be honest, if you do and he keeps coming back for more, doesn't that mean something?"

I thought about what she said for a moment then slowly nodded. "You were always the more level-headed of the two of us. I don't know how I managed without you for all these years."

"Just listen to your gut, Cassie. That's all I'm saying."

"I'll try," I said. "You know me, I overthink things and I can't help that. I can't just listen to my gut. But, for you, I'll try."

Ashley laughed and opened the door to the restaurant.

"I'll have to tell you all about how Xander and I started dating one day. Let's just say I'm not always level-headed," she said. "Now let's get back inside before they send out a search party for us."

Chapter Seven
Cassie

"Cassie? Cassie, you up?" Becca said.

Becca's voice came through the thin vinyl door. I was still in bed, but it slowly dawned on me why she was there. Somehow after dinner with Ashley and her friends, I had completely forgotten that Gabriel said his driver, Stan, was going to arrange for movers in the morning.

I grabbed the black yoga pants I had dropped on the floor before going to bed and pulled them on. As I slid open the door, I grabbed an oversized purple sweatshirt that was on top of my dresser.

Becca was in her restaurant clothes, jeans and a T-shirt with a red and white trolley on it. Her light brown hair was pulled back into a messy bun. With her hair back like that, her freckles became more pronounced. She always worked Saturdays at the restaurant so she could make more tips.

"I'm so sorry, Becca. I went to bed before you got home and should've left you a note. Gabriel wants me to move into his apartment."

"Wait a sec, your boss?" she asked, her eyebrows shooting up. "You haven't even gone on a date and he wants you to move in? Wow, you must be some kisser!"

"Yeah, I know, crazy right? He was here yesterday and I don't know what happened, but he said I can't live here. He said his apartment is near the gym so I wouldn't even need a car, I could walk."

"Really? Where the gym is? That's a pretty swanky area. You might want to check it out. What's the worst that could happen? It'll beat the hell out of living here."

"You're nuts," I said, laughing. "I can't move in with him. I barely know him."

"Well, there are movers here and they look like they're ready to work. If you're not moving, maybe Gabriel won't mind if I moved in," she said with a big grin.

I went down the stairs and opened the apartment door. Stan was standing outside. Beyond the open main door of the building, I could see a small moving truck with two men waiting on the sidewalk.

"Good morning, Miss," Stan said. "I'm sorry if we're a bit early, but I thought you might like the day to relax and get settled in after the move."

"I'm not moving, Stan. I barely know Gabriel and he's my boss. I can't move in with him."

Stan laughed. "I believe you misunderstood, Miss. Mr. Kohl doesn't live there, this *was* his apartment. He hasn't lived in the penthouse for at least four years. Before you make up your mind, why don't you at least come and see the place?"

Stan caught me by surprise. Behind me, Becca pushed her way through the door, put her arm around my shoulders, and smiled.

"That's a great idea, Cassie," she said. "You should check the place out, it could be perfect." Looking at Stan, she tilted her head to the side. "So Stan, what's he charging her for rent?"

"There is no rent," he said. "Mr. Kohl said there would be no expenses."

"Seriously?" She pushed me back inside the apartment and lowered her voice. "You have to take this. Listen, I love having you here, but there's no way I'm gonna let you pass this up." She stuck her head out the door and looked at Stan directly. "Where's your ride, Stan? Let's see this place."

I couldn't argue with Becca. I'd be stupid to not take advantage of this opportunity, but it didn't feel right. Just what I could save from rent alone would make a huge difference in my life, but I couldn't live there rent free. That wasn't like me at all.

I had convinced myself that Canyon Cove was going to be where my life would turn around. But I didn't think it had anything to do with an apartment or even a man. The city gave me what I came here for--a job. I didn't need a fancy place, but I was curious to see where Gabriel lived.

Becca and I grabbed our bags and locked the door to our apartment. Stan had a folded wad of bills in his hand and he gave each of the movers some cash then patted them on the back. He walked over to a nearby dark blue sedan and opened the two passenger doors at once, then motioned for Becca and I to get in.

"I told the guys to go get some breakfast," he said. "They'll be back in about an hour. I figure that's enough time for you to see the place and make your decision."

Everything was moving so fast I didn't feel like myself. Things like this didn't happen in real life. I felt like I was watching a movie, and I couldn't wait to see what was going to happen next.

The car sped in and out of traffic as it made its way to the downtown area of the city. Stan slowed down and pulled up in front of a tall glass building in the shape of an obelisk that reflected the sky. As he stopped the car, a doorman in a European-styled navy suit with a long coat stepped forward and opened the car doors. Becca and I stepped out as Stan handed the doorman the keys to the car, then motioned for us to enter the building.

As we walked towards the ornate front doors with contemporary iron design work over the glass, another doorman appeared and opened them for us. I stopped as soon as I stepped into the lobby. I had never seen anything like it before.

The lobby was wide with tall square columns that held up a coffered ceiling with hidden lights, which made it look like it was glowing. Everything was marble, from the ivory-colored walls to the black and white Art Deco style flooring. The columns created open rooms with black leather chairs on top of pale blue rugs. Decorative sconces hung on the walls.

Stan waited for Becca and me by the elevator as we looked around. As the glass elevator rose, we were able to see the skyline of Canyon Cove, including the Great Park.

"Wow, how far up are we going?" Becca asked.

"To the top," Stan said. "The 51st floor. The apartment is two floors, four bedrooms, with a view of the entire city."

"This is ridiculous. I don't need this apartment and I definitely don't need that much space. I don't belong here," I said. "I'm sorry for wasting your time."

"Shut up, Cassie," Becca said. "Just take a look at the place. You don't have to stay. Come on, I know you're curious."

The elevator slowed to a stop and the doors opened to a white marble hallway similar to the lobby. Stan walked towards one of the two tall dark wooden doors, put in the key, and swung the door open before motioning for Becca and me to enter.

The first thing I noticed when we entered the apartment was the wide plank distressed wood floor that stretched out beyond the wide entryway to the dining room ahead of us. Just past the dining room were floor-to-ceiling glass windows.

As we followed Stan further in, the apartment opened up. The room ahead of us was the dining room, which shared the space with the living room and its two-story glass walls with a view of the park.

"Holy crap," I whispered.

"You could say that again," Becca said.

We walked over to the windows and as I stood in front of it, I felt the cold emanating from the glass. I looked down the length of the building but had to step back when I felt dizzy.

I couldn't believe the view and couldn't pull myself away from it. As I admired all the different buildings and the large rectangular Great Park in the middle of everything, I wondered if I could see mine and Becca's apartment from here.

"As you can see, the apartment is furnished," Stan said. "The only things you'll really need are your clothing and some groceries. A library rounds out this floor. If you're ready, I can take you upstairs to see the bedrooms."

Forcing myself to turn away from the view of the city, I noticed a large room on the other side of the dining room that I assumed was the kitchen. I was probably more curious to see the library than the bedrooms, but it didn't matter. I had already made my decision. I didn't need to see any more.

"I can't do this, Stan. I told Gabriel yesterday I wasn't moving, and I meant it."

"He told me you would say that," he said as he pulled out his phone, tapped it, and held it up to his ear. Stan came closer to me and I could hear the ringing, then Gabriel's muffled voice.

"Yes, Stan, she said no, didn't she?" Gabriel said.

Stan handed the phone to me and eyes wide, I knew what was going to happen. Gabriel would convince me to stay even though I didn't want to.

"Cassie, it's Gabriel. I know what you're thinking, and I'm not in the position to argue with you right now. Promise you'll stay the weekend and we'll discuss this on Monday."

"No, this isn't right. You have to let me pay rent or something. I can't just live here for free."

He sighed, sounding frustrated. "You work for me, right?"

"Yes, but what does this have to do with work?"

"You've just been hired to housesit for me."

"That's ridiculous."

"If you don't accept your added responsibility, I'll have to fire you."

"You don't mean that," I said.

"Do you want to test me?"

"No," I said, giving in.

"I told you, you don't have a choice. If you want to consider this interim housing, fine. But I will not sit by while you live in that hovel," he said sternly before his voice softened. "Cassie, I'm only doing this because I care about you."

My heart thumped in my chest when I heard his words. He hung up before I could say anything, but it didn't matter. Whatever Gabriel's reason for pushing me to stay there, he won. I was giving in. And as much as I wanted to fight it, I was falling for him.

***

That evening, after the movers and Becca had left, I watched the sky change colors as the sun set. I was so overwhelmed by everything that I didn't even take notice of the furniture or anything else in the apartment. Now that I was alone, I decided to look around.

I kicked my sneakers off by the marble fireplace in the living room, then walked barefoot on the soft, light gray rug towards a tan and ivory curved couch. Sitting down, I ran my hand over the expensive fabric of the seats.

Turning around, I looked at the long black rectangular table with chrome legs in the dining room. The table was surrounded by ten tan leather chairs with chrome accents. The table and chairs stood on a large oval rug similar to the one in the living room. Above the table hung five lights with glass blown fixtures. A white wall blocked my view of the kitchen, but from where I was sitting, I could see a large built-in stainless steel refrigerator unlike anything I had seen in a home before.

Part of me wanted to run around the apartment and take in as much as I could as quickly as possible, but I still couldn't believe I was there. I stayed on the couch, nervous that if I stepped into another room, I'd wake up and realize it was all just a dream.

I was used to living in places like the apartment I had lived in with Becca. I learned early on that anything too good to be true usually was. But what was the catch here? When was the clock going to strike midnight and change the apartment into a pumpkin?

As night fell, the lights automatically came on and gave the room a warm glow. My stomach rumbled loudly and I realized I didn't know where to go for food. I picked up my phone, ready to call Becca, until I remembered it was Saturday night and she was working.

I walked into the kitchen to look around, hoping there was a can of soup or something left from when Gabriel lived there. As my feet padded along on the cold white tile floor, I heard the front door unlock. My first instinct was to hide, so I ducked near one of the oversized islands. It didn't occur to me that whoever was entering the apartment was using a key, only that someone was coming in.

I stood up and moved closer to the kitchen doorway to see who was there, but I couldn't see anyone. I knew they were going to walk through the doorway soon. The clacking of shoes on the wooden floor grew louder as they entered the dining room and my heart beat even faster.

Hanging over the island next to me were several pots and pans. I reached up and unhooked a frying pan, then held it back over my shoulder, ready to wallop whoever was entering the kitchen. I tightened my grip around the handle of the frying pan as the footsteps came closer. I was too afraid to look, so I closed my eyes and swung with all my might.

"Get out of here, you fucking son of a bitch," I screamed as I swung my body with the frying pan.

The pan was yanked out of my hands, and with a clang, it dropped to the floor. My eyes flew open as I was spun around and strong arms wrapped around me from behind, pinning my arms to my sides.

"I always knew you were feisty," Gabriel said.

I breathed out a sigh of relief, happy to hear his voice. As I relaxed, he kissed my neck and I melted against him.

"You can't just barge in on a woman like that. I could've really hurt you."

"I don't think so," he said with a laugh.

Gabriel let go of me as he laughed. I spun around to look at him, annoyed by his arrogance. He was wearing a charcoal gray suit that was perfectly tailored for his body.

As he continued laughing at me, he took his suit jacket off and folded it delicately over one of the dining room chairs. I wanted to yell at him just for the hell of it, to knock him down from his high horse a bit, but at the sight of him in his perfect suit with his crisp white button-down shirt that hugged his shoulders and biceps, my anger drifted away.

Tilting his head towards me, Gabriel smiled. He started rolling up the sleeves of his shirt when the doorbell rang.

"Good thing I got here before the delivery boy," he said. "I can only imagine the damage you would've done to him."

"Delivery? What did you order? This place has everything."

"Everything but food," he said, opening the door.

On the other side of the door was a skinny boy with messy blond hair who couldn't be more than sixteen years old. His eyes lit up as he recognized Gabriel. Gabriel took the bags from him, put them down on top of the foyer table, then reached into his pocket and pulled out his wallet.

"Oh no, man, you don't need to tip me. Just tell me how I can get a shot in the MMAC," the boy said.

"You just have to work hard," Gabriel said as he shoved a hundred dollar bill into the boy's hands. "Have a good night."

Gabriel closed the door, picked up the groceries, and brought them into the kitchen.

"I figured with the move you didn't have enough time to go shopping," he said. "If you need anything else, just call the store. Tell them what you want and give them this address. Everything will be charged to me."

"You don't have to do that. I can buy my own groceries."

"As long as you're living in my home, you won't pay for anything."

Gabriel had a way of leaving me speechless. I opened my mouth, ready to argue with him again, but then I noticed the tender look in his eyes. He stepped closer to me and his large hands cupped my face. He kissed my forehead gently and tilted my face towards him.

My breath caught in my throat. In my mind, I had relived the kiss in the locker room so many times I almost thought it was a dream. I closed my eyes as his lips came down upon mine.

His hand slipped down and pressed my body tighter against him. As I wrapped my arms around his shoulders, I tilted my head, wanting more of the kiss.

As I moved my tongue to meet his, he picked me up and sat me on the counter. He lifted my sweatshirt off me, leaving me in my bra, and leaned me back so I was lying on the cold granite.

"I've wanted you from the moment I saw you," he said.

His hand slid over my shoulder, moving my bra strap down as his lips closed over mine. His kiss became more demanding as I unbuttoned his shirt. I reached the last button, then pulled away from his kiss to admire his muscular torso, but just as I was going to move my hand up his smooth chest, the doorbell rang.

Gabriel's brow wrinkled, looking confused. As he lowered his head to kiss me, the doorbell rang again.

"I'm sorry," he said, shaking his head. "Maybe it's that kid again or the doorman."

He walked out of the kitchen and I hopped down from the countertop and pulled my sweatshirt back on.

"This better be good," I muttered as I followed him to the door.

Gabriel opened the door and a woman with long dark hair in a short, skintight, amber-colored dress smiled as she held up a bottle of wine.

"I knew you couldn't stay out in the country for too long," she said. "I missed you. Even if you never called like you promised to."

Looking at her with her perfect make-up and slutty clothes, I wished I had changed out of my yoga pants and sweatshirt from earlier. But then I realized it didn't matter what either of us was wearing, I was in his apartment, not her.

With Gabriel's hand still on the door, I slipped under his arm and then put my arm around his waist and stroked his bare chest with my hand. I gave the woman a big smile, then looked up at Gabriel and batted my eyelashes.

"Honey, you didn't tell me we were having guests tonight," I said, smiling.

"Cassie, this is Monica. She lives at the other end of the hall," Gabriel said as he took the bottle of wine from Monica. "Oh, a Cab. You know how much I love a good Cab. This is a very generous gift, Monica. Cassie just moved in today."

As Gabriel pushed the door closed, Monica started to speak, but he ignored her and kept his arm around me.

Walking back towards the kitchen, his cell phone rang, stopping him. He pulled the phone out of his pants pocket and a name flashed across the screen, but I couldn't make it out. Gabriel hesitated as he looked at his phone. I thought he was going to answer it, but then he looked at me and put the phone away.

We went back into the kitchen and he set the bottle of wine on the counter. I was a little jealous seeing that Mack was right about Gabriel being a player but quickly convinced myself it was in the past. After seeing Monica though, I wondered what Gabriel saw in me. I knew I was pretty, but even on a good day I never looked that perfect. If all his women looked like her, I couldn't compete. Plus I didn't want to compete. The more I was near him, the more I wanted him for myself.

As I put the groceries away, Gabriel's phone chimed. He took the phone out and held it up to his ear. I tried to pretend that it didn't bother me, but I couldn't help myself, it did. Even without knowing who it was, I was jealous. Who else would call him late on a Saturday night? It had to be a woman.

While I finished putting the groceries away, I strained to hear a voice from voicemail, but I couldn't hear anything. My insides felt like they were burning from my jealousy. I was being stupid. He was there with me, not with someone else. If I said it to myself enough, maybe I'd believe it.

Gabriel sent a text, then his phone beeped as he got a text back. He sighed then put the phone back in his pocket and stared past me, like I wasn't there. I tried to catch his gaze but his eyes darted away.

"Thank you for letting me live here," I said, trying to bring him back from wherever it was he went. "And thanks for the food. I love cooking. You'll have to let me make you dinner sometime. It's the least I can do to make it up to you."

"Thanks, but I'll have to pass. You were right yesterday, I'm your boss. That would be inappropriate."

"But…I don't understand," I said.

I shook my head, trying to clear the confusion from my brain. *What just happened?* I followed him as he walked into the dining room.

"Just yesterday you asked me out on a date," I said. "And not even ten minutes ago your tongue was down my throat."

"A lot can happen in ten minutes," he said, picking up his jacket. "Just look at a fight. In ten minutes, a guy who is getting the shit beat out of him can knock the other guy out or grab hold of the guy and submit him. In my business, ten minutes can make or break a career."

"But this isn't MMA, this isn't a fight, and this is definitely not business. Tell me, did something happen? Did I do something?"

"No, it's not you. It's just the way it is and we should keep it business between us."

Gabriel took several long strides to the door. It didn't matter what I said and there was nothing I could do, his mind was made up. He stood in the doorway and looked at me, our eyes finally meeting. There was something behind his blue eyes, but he turned away before I knew what it was.

As he closed the door behind him, I decided this wasn't how I wanted it to end. The other day he said I didn't have a choice, but he was wrong.

I didn't want to see him at work and think about what if. I didn't want my memories of his kiss to be all that was left. And I didn't want to live in his apartment if it meant I wouldn't see him except as my boss.

Rushing to the door, I pulled it open, hoping the elevator wasn't there. Gabriel was standing in front of the elevator doors with his cell phone to his ear.

"I'm on my way. I have to go," he said before putting his phone back in his pocket.

"You can't just leave like this," I said. "You can't just ignore what this is between us."

"It's complicated, Cassie. You wouldn't understand and even if you did, I'm not sure I want you to."

"Just tell me two things, Gabriel. Did that kiss mean anything to you?"

He smiled as he cradled my face in his hand and ran his thumb over my chin. The elevator chimed as the doors opened.

"You have no idea what it meant to me," he said. "But now isn't the right time."

"Then when is?"

"You said you wanted me to tell you two things. Is that your second question?"

I swallowed hard, thinking about my second question. I had to ask it.

"Who called?" I asked.

For a moment Gabriel looked surprised, then just as quickly his face turned to stone and he stepped away from me. He entered the elevator then turned to face me.

"That's none of your business," he said, then pressed the button to close the elevator doors.

I went back into the apartment feeling more confused and lost than ever. Just as I was afraid of, the clock struck midnight and my fairy tale was over.

Chapter Eight
Gabriel

I closed my eyes and leaned against the cool glass wall of the elevator. Cassie's kiss awakened feelings I had forgotten about, feelings that were better off left for dead. This wasn't how I wanted things to work out with her. I wanted more, but I made the right decision when I ended it before things got serious.

I had to do it. Getting that phone call made me realize how complicated things really were. Cassie deserved better. She deserved someone who could put her on a pedestal and give her one hundred percent of his attention. I had too many things going on and was being pulled in too many directions. Things were easier when I didn't commit to one woman.

The elevator opened in the underground garage where I had parked my burgundy Porsche Cayenne. As I wound my way out of Canyon Cove's downtown, my phone rang. It could only be one person. I thought about letting the call go to voicemail but then decided to answer.

"I told you, I'm on my way home," I said.

"Geez, calm down. I wasn't going to ask," Gideon, my brother, said.

"Sorry, I thought you were--"

"Ahh yes," he said, interrupting me. "You know, I never imagined you with an old ball and chain."

"What do you want?"

"Okay, okay, I can see you can't take a joke. Rough night?"

"Gideon, you've never been one for small talk, what do you want?"

The phone was quiet for a moment so I looked over to make sure the call was still connected. I loved my younger brother, but he had a lot of growing up to do.

"I met someone," he said, sounding serious.

"So? You know as well as I do, us Kohls don't settle down."

"You did," he said.

"That's different," I said as my mind wandered to Cassie.

"And so is this. I think I'm in love."

"You've been in love before and I've never gotten a phone call."

"Fine, I need money, okay?"

"I just wanted the truth," I said. "What happened to the money I sent you?"

"That was for tuition and books."

"I sent you enough to cover your meal plan, too."

"You did, but there's this girl," he said dreamily.

"Got it. Have you thought about getting a job? I worked at the gym while I was in college."

"I'm thinking about dropping out."

"You can't drop out, you need a degree."

"You dropped out," he said. "And look at you. You wouldn't be where you're at right now if you stayed in school."

"School wasn't right for me, I was a fighter. What are you doing?"

"I don't know, I'm just not cut out for this, Gabe. I know what you're trying to do and all, but college just isn't me. Maybe there's something I can do at your gym. You're always busy in the main office being Mr. Corporate nowadays anyway."

"Actually, I've been spending more time at the gym."

"Oh? New ring girl?"

"No, she's not a ring girl."

"Hmm, but she *is* a girl. What's she doing there?"

"She's working for Mack. She's his team's physical therapist."

"Sounds hot. Maybe I should work at the gym and help her out," he said with a laugh.

"I don't want you anywhere near her," I said.

"You sound serious."

"I don't know, Gideon. There's something about her. She's different."

"See, that's exactly how I feel about Julie. I mean Janey. Shit, what's her name again?"

"Never mind, Gideon. Think about school. You're a smart guy, you shouldn't let that go to waste. Call me next week and let me know what you've decided."

I hung up with the memory of being just like my younger brother not that long ago. I never had a hard time getting women and after the MMAC took off, it became even easier. I knew what those ring girls and women like Monica were after--my money. Cassie wasn't like that.

As I turned into the driveway, the iron gates clanked then opened slowly. Ahead of me was the estate I bought four years ago when I decided my bachelor pad days were over. I don't know why I kept the apartment except that maybe it was my way of clinging to the past. A past when my life was much less complicated.

As I pulled into the garage, loneliness crept over me. I was wrong when I told Cassie we couldn't be together. I needed to give things with her a chance. As I got out of my car, I thought about the sweet taste of her lips. I had to make things right with Cassie if I wanted to taste her again.

As I entered the kitchen from the garage, my cell phone rang again. I sighed when I saw who was calling before I answered it.

"I'm home," I said before hanging up.

Karen entered the kitchen, her face angry as she narrowed her eyes at me. Her dark hair had streaks of grey in it and it was pulled back into a low ponytail.

"You said if anything happened to call and you'd be right back," she said.

"Karen, we need to talk," I said.

"What if it was an emergency? It took you thirty minutes to get here from when I called. And you didn't even answer."

"Because I knew it wasn't an emergency. I was downtown. I came back as quickly as I could."

"Well, it wasn't fast enough."

"You know what, Karen? I don't need this. Pack up your things. I want you gone by morning."

She stormed out of the room and then I heard a door slam. She didn't have many things, but I knew she would take her time packing. It had happened before, it would happen again.

Sighing, I went upstairs. I stood in front of the closed bedroom door and listened. A radio played music on the other side. I knocked on the door, then opened it slowly before entering the room.

She was lying on her stomach, twirling her ponytail with her finger. Looking up at me, she gave me a big smile, then folded the corner of the page of the book she was reading. She was the most beautiful girl in the world.

"Hey, sweetie, I'm sorry it took me so long to get home. Are you okay?"

"I'm fine, Daddy," she said as she sat up. "I told you not to rush home in my text."

"I know, but Karen was going crazy."

"Tell me about it. I was here."

"What happened?" I asked.

"Dakota called and Karen freaked out. She said the cell phone was only for emergencies. She didn't care that I hadn't spoken to Dakota in two weeks."

"Now, Wendy, you know I don't like it when you call her that."

"I know, sorry. Mom called."

"Is she okay?"

"Who knows," she said. "I'm not even sure where she is. I mean she sounds happy, but you know how she is."

"I do," I said, pulling Wendy in for a hug. "Just always remember she loves you."

"I know, but I still miss her. At least I have you."

"I'll always be here for you no matter what," I said as I stood beside her bed.

"Dad? Aren't you lonely?"

I turned back to look at my little girl and forced a smile. I didn't want her to see my loneliness. Time for myself could wait until she was much older. She had already been through enough.

"You know, you're very mature for a nine year old," I said, laughing.

"Living with Dakota will do that. I mean Mom. You know, she tells me to call her Dakota."

"If you're talking to me about her, you're calling her Mom. Understand?"

She nodded.

"You didn't always travel with her. I don't know if she ever told you, but I was there when you were born. The three of us lived together the first year of your life, but you know how your mom is. She can't stay anywhere for too long."

"I know, she told me you were the only father I ever knew and the best one she could ever hope for for me."

"I'm sure you remember staying with me once you were a little older," I said.

She nodded. "I had my own bedroom in the glass apartment. I loved when we stayed with you. I got to pretend we were a family."

Sadness blanketed me as I heard Wendy's words. She deserved to have a family. Instead, she had a free spirit for a mother, and me. Dakota wanted Wendy to have a stable life and she knew I had the money to give her anything she desired. Dakota couldn't change, she needed to go wherever the wind blew her. Wendy deserved better than that.

"You know, I love your mother very much. I always have," I said.

"I know, but you're not *in* love with her."

"Do you even know what that means?" I asked, laughing.

"I've seen some movies, I think I get it," she said, grinning.

Four years ago I gladly signed the papers adopting Wendy, but in the back of my mind I always wanted us to live as a family. I did love Dakota, but Wendy was right, I wasn't in love with her. I'm not sure I ever was.

The first time I truly fell in love was when I saw that little red-faced baby in the blue and pink striped hospital blanket. Wendy was perfect, and I gladly changed my world when she became mine. I left behind all the women who meant nothing to me. I bought an estate in the country so Wendy could go outside and play. And I kept her a secret so that she would be safe.

But I was lonely. And it wasn't until I met Cassie that I realized how lonely I really was. I wanted to get to know her better, but I didn't know if I could. I wanted to be there for Wendy and have dinner with her every night. But the more I got to know Cassie, I imagined her there with us, too.

It was a lot to take on for anyone. It wasn't just me, I had a daughter and she would always come first. I wanted a woman who would love Wendy as if she was her own, but I didn't know if that was possible. *Did women like that exist?* I knew none of the women I had dated before would. I wasn't even sure about Dakota and she was Wendy's mother. But Cassie was different, and I wanted to give her a chance.

I also wanted to take things slow. Whatever I did had to be right not just for me and Cassie, but for Wendy too. Cassie and I needed time together before I could tell her about Wendy. I didn't want to lose her, but for us to have a chance I had to keep some things secret. It was the only way I could know for certain that she really was the one.

I had to be cautious. I couldn't trust myself when it came to women. I had made too many wrong decisions and had learned the hard way that people weren't always what they seemed. Dakota was a prime example of that, but I never faulted her. If it wasn't for her, I wouldn't have Wendy in my life. And I wouldn't have become the man I was today.

Nine Years Ago

As I smeared the blood from my cheek with the back of my glove, I looked across the cage. Coach was yelling at me, but I couldn't hear his words. I was too focused on the man on the other side of the ring.

I took a sip of water and swallowed. The cut wasn't a big deal, just a lucky punch. It was underneath my eye and happened all the time because of my cheekbones.

Coach bent down so his face was inches from mine as he wiped my glove. This fight had to end quick, I needed to go. Dakota needed me.

"You've gone soft, Kohl," Coach said. "This fight should have been over by now. You know better than to stand up with a boxer."

He was right, but my head wasn't in it, it was at the hospital with Dakota where she was in labor. As much as I loved to fight, being there was the last place I wanted to be. I knew what I had to do though. It was time to dig in deep and end the match. I wasn't going to settle for the loser's earnings.

The bell rang and it was just two fighters in the cage again. It didn't matter who my opponent was, I was going to beat him.

A left hook came towards my cheek, but I ducked under and managed a double leg takedown, making him fall. A quick hammerfist to his face was enough for him to turn onto his side, giving me his back.

Wrapping my legs around, I dug my heels into his thighs for back control. He tried to twist, to spin out of my grasp, but my hooks were in deep. I could feel his movements quicken. He was nervous. One small mistake and I would finish him.

My chance came when he lifted his chin. Keeping my hand flat, I slid it underneath his chin, making room for my arm as it followed. His neck was caught between my bicep and my forearm. He jerked back, trying to headbutt me, but it only let me sink my arm in further.

I pulled my shoulders back, tightening the choke hold, and in seconds I felt his hand tapping my elbow. The ref waved, ending the fight, giving me the win by submission.

After my arm was raised, I went back to the locker rooms where Coach cut the wraps from my hand. I was anxious to leave and get to the hospital, but glad that the fight earned me enough to pay for the things the baby and Dakota would need.

As I slipped a sweatshirt over my head, my opponent's trainer entered the room. Wearing a cardigan sweater with his white hair brushed back, he didn't look like much, but Mack Draven was known as one of the best trainers around. However, if he wanted to talk to me, he would have to wait.

"Good fight, Kohl," Mack said. "I knew it was over as soon as he threw the left."

"Thanks," I said. "I can't talk right now though."

"That's fine, I know how it is. Here's my card. Gimme a call sometime."

I took the card from him and shoved it into my pocket as I left. The clock was ticking on Dakota and her baby. I hadn't wanted to leave her alone at the hospital, but I didn't have a choice, I needed to earn money.

Taking a cab to the hospital, I rushed to the maternity ward and a nurse brought me to Dakota's room. The room was dark and Dakota's eyes were closed. I turned to the nurse, who smiled as she put her hand on my arm.

"It's a girl," she whispered.

"Is she okay? Where is she?" I asked.

"She's perfect. Dakota asked for her to be taken to the nursery shortly after she was born."

"When was this?"

"Less than an hour ago."

I hated that I missed it, but we needed the money. I followed the nurse to the nursery where several babies were asleep. She motioned for me to sit on a white wooden rocking chair in the corner as she rolled a bassinet towards me.

"Say hello to your daughter," she said.

"Did Dakota choose a name?"

"No, she said you would."

The nurse picked up the baby and placed her in my arms. I stared down at this tiny flushed creature with black fuzz on her head. I couldn't believe how fragile and delicate she was. Earlier I was cutting off the blood supply to a man with these arms, and now I held a sleeping baby.

Her eyes fluttered open and she looked directly at me. The nurse came back with a tiny bottle of formula and put it in my hands.

"She's been looking around a lot. She's very alert," she said.

The nurse left us alone as I began to feed her. My heart felt heavy as I thought about this baby coming into the world alone. I did what I had to do, but things were going to be different.

"I will always be here for you," I whispered. "Whatever happens, whatever you need, I will be here for you always."

Her eyelids fluttered closed as she drank. I lifted my arm slightly and gently kissed her forehead as I breathed in her baby scent. Everything I did from that moment on was going to be for her.

As she slept in my arms, I looked around the nursery. On the wall was a collage of nursery rhyme and story images. A flying pirate ship caught my eye and I smiled as her name came to me. I set the empty bottle aside and stroked her plump cheek.

"I love you, Wendy."

Present Day

"Daddy? Hello, Dad!"

I blinked as I focused back on Wendy lying on her bed. It seemed like no time had passed since she was born, yet in front of me was a girl and not a baby. I smiled at her as I pushed a stray hair out of her eyes.

"Sorry, I was thinking," I said.

"About what?"

"How would you feel if I started dating?" I asked. "I promise I won't take any time away from you. I'll still be there to pick you up from school and we'll still have dinner every night."

"You met someone, didn't you? When can I meet her? What's her name?" she asked excitedly.

"Cassie," I said with a smile.

First thing Monday I would make things right with Cassie and if I was lucky, she'd finally say yes to a date.

Chapter Nine

Cassie

I spent the rest of the weekend playing over in my head what I was going to say to Gabriel the next time I saw him. The more I thought about it, the angrier I got.

Wearing a pair of black pants I thought hugged my ass nicely and a teal blouse that showed off a little cleavage, I walked the block from the apartment to the gym. I wanted to make sure that I looked good when I told Gabriel that I did have a choice.

Gabriel's limo drove past and stopped in front of the gym. Gabriel got out and turned towards me. I was surprised to see him arrive at the gym in a suit and had to force myself to not mentally undress him. The nice thing about the gym was getting to see him half naked a lot of the time.

As I approached, he gave me a crooked smile with a look I remembered from the locker room. Staying angry at him was going to be harder than I thought.

"You look stunning," he said.

"Don't talk to me like that. You said you wanted to keep things professional, remember?"

He opened the side door to the gym and held it open as I entered.

"We need to talk," he said as I walked past him.

No! I thought. *This has to be on my terms.*

"Maybe later," I said. "I'm very busy."

"Now," he said as he moved his hand to my lower back and guided me to his office.

I folded my arms in front of me and tapped my foot as Gabriel closed his office door. He stood in front of me and lowered his head to my height.

"Now isn't the time for short jokes," I said as I turned my back towards him.

I wasn't really angry with him anymore, but I didn't want him thinking he got off that easily. He needed to learn he couldn't change his mind about me from one day to the next. I wasn't a toy or a game for him to play. That might have worked with his other women, but I was going to be different.

"Cassie, please listen to me. I've been doing a lot of thinking the past couple of days."

"Good for you."

"And I made a mistake."

"Wait. What?" I said, spinning around to face him.

"I made a mistake when I said we shouldn't be together. Since that first day when you yelled at that fighter, I knew you were different. I knew you were special. But there's something I need to tell you."

He took my hand and pulled out a chair from in front of his desk. As I sat down, he sat on the edge of his desk in front of me.

"Is this about the women? There's someone else, isn't there? Mack warned me about you. Is that what it is?"

"No, it's not that. All of that is in the past. I'm not that man anymore and haven't been in a long time," he said quietly. "But there is someone else."

My heart sank into my stomach. I was glad I was sitting when he said that because I was sure I would have fallen over.

Gabriel stroked his chin as he paced the room. I was waiting for his big reveal--he was married. Or maybe he had a fiancée, or a live-in girlfriend in his big mansion or wherever it was he lived.

The longer he paced, the more anxious I got. I couldn't take the silence anymore.

"I'm moving out," I said as I rose to my feet. "I never wanted to live in that big ass apartment in the first place. And I'm sorry, but I think it's disgusting that you keep a place in the city like that. How many other women have you moved in before me?"

Gabriel looked stunned. I guessed he never had a woman say anything back to him about it before.

"Cassie--"

"No, just stop," I said, interrupting him. "Do not answer that question because I really do not want to know the answer. I'm leaving."

I stormed out the door as my legs shook underneath me. I felt weak and vulnerable, but I hoped he didn't see any of that. His memory of me had to be that I was strong.

"Cassie Monroe," Gabriel's voice boomed in the hall. "I am not done talking."

His voice stopped me and I spun on my heel to face him. I was so angry that my hands were curled up into fists at my side and I shook with rage.

"I've heard enough," I said.

"Do you want to hit me?" he said as he walked down the hall towards me. "Would that make you feel better? You didn't give me a chance to explain."

"You said there's someone else!"

"I chose the wrong words."

"That's exactly what a cheater would say. You're just playing games with me," I said as my fist shot into his stomach.

His eyes widened as his hands covered his stomach. He had a twinkle in his eyes that made me want to punch him even harder.

"You hit me," he said, laughing.

"You deserved it," I said.

I turned away from him and walked as fast as I could towards my office. *Is he following me? Is he still laughing at me?* There was no way I was turning around to find out.

Entering my office, I closed the door behind me and leaned against it as I dropped my face into my hands. I felt ridiculous, asinine. I had never felt so out of control or unlike me as I did these few weeks I had been working at the gym. But I never felt as at ease as I did when I was with him.

I was sure he would follow me. Any minute now I would hear his knock. Any second now I would hear his footsteps. Any second now...but I didn't hear anything except for the casters of my chair against the floor.

Opening my eyes, I peeked through my fingers. Gabriel was sitting at my desk.

"How the hell did you get here before me?" I demanded as I crossed the room to him.

He pointed to a door in the corner opposite my desk. A door I had always assumed was a closet.

"That's my office," he said. "Now please sit and listen to me. That's all I'm asking."

He looked pitiful. His eyes were tender and his face soft. I knew whatever he had to say, he had no intention of hurting me. This was a man who cared about me. He held his hand out to me, and I placed my hand in his and everything felt right.

"You're in my chair," I said with a grin.

He tugged me onto his lap and pulled me close. As he tilted his head towards me, I moved my hand onto his broad shoulder, over his suit jacket.

Our eyes met and he smiled before kissing my lips. He touched my cheek then pushed my hair back, over my shoulder, and kissed my neck before his lips traveled up towards my ear.

"If you were in a skirt right now, I'd have my way with you," he whispered as he squeezed my thigh.

"Not here," I said, giggling. "I didn't even know about your secret door there, for all I know, I'm being recorded too."

"The door was right there. How did you not see a door?" he said, laughing. "Fine, then not here. Let me do this right then. Seeing you every day has made me forget one simple thing. We still haven't gone on a date. So how about a late dinner Friday night?"

"Why wait until Friday? Worried about school the next day?" I joked.

"You could say that," he said.

"Okay, well, I know it's my fault we haven't been on a date yet, so how about I make you dinner?"

"Only if you let me take care of dessert," he said with a raise of his eyebrows and a smirk.

"It's a deal," I said.

"Cassie, about what I said before--"

"No, I don't want to hear it. Not now," I said. "Just tell me, can I trust you?"

"Absolutely."

"Then that's all I need to know."

The look on his face was enough to tell me he was being honest and that I could trust him. It didn't matter what Mack said about him or how he ran out that night at his apartment, it didn't even matter that he said there was someone else.

Thinking about his words, I remembered him saying he wasn't that man anymore. I couldn't believe one thing and ignore the other, but I trusted him. Deep down I knew he meant it when he said he chose the wrong words, and that was all that mattered. He would tell me everything when he was ready.

Chapter Ten

Cassie

"Dammit! Why does time have to move so fast," I said, looking at the clock in the kitchen.

It was almost time for Gabriel to arrive and I wasn't dressed. I ran up the stairs, through the master bedroom, and into the bathroom where I hung my favorite dress. It was a burgundy-colored halter dress with a flared skirt that ended just above my knee.

Every time I wore it I looked fabulous, but it had been a long time. The dress had been folded in a box for months since I didn't have a closet at Becca's. Had I been thinking, I would have had it dry cleaned so it would look perfect for Gabriel. Instead, I had the shower running on hot so the steam would take the wrinkles out. I didn't trust myself with an iron.

As I tugged on the soft fabric, my phone rang. Glancing over, I saw 'Mom' flitting across the screen.

"Crap! She's got the worst timing," I said before answering. "Hi, Mom, I don't have a lot of time."

"Of course you don't," she said. "Ever since you moved to that damned place, you never have any time for your mother."

"What are you talking about? We still talk every day."

"Well, it's not enough. I haven't seen you in months."

"I know and I'm sorry, but Crosswicks is a little far for just a day trip."

"Then spend the weekend," she said. "Or better yet, a week. Are you coming home for the holidays?"

"Umm, about that."

"What? Don't tell me I'm not going to see my baby for Christmas."

"Please don't be dramatic, Mom," I said, knowing that was impossible for her. "I don't have any vacation time yet and I wanted to save some more money."

"Work? That again? What about your friend there, that man you told me about. Isn't he your boss? You can't blow him or something for a few paid days off?"

"Mother!" I said, surprised to hear her speak like that.

"What? Back in my day, they called me--"

"No, I do *not* want to hear that. Please stop."

"Suit yourself," she said. "Maybe I sheltered you too much. Your cousin Ashley bagged herself a billionaire in Canyon Cove. Maybe she got the Monroe gene you're obviously missing."

"I'm not going to talk about sex with my mother."

"I was a popular girl back in the day, that's all I'm saying."

I shook my head, glad we weren't having this conversation in person.

"Can we talk about something else?" I asked.

"Something else? I thought you said you didn't have time for me."

"I didn't say that. I said I didn't have a lot of time. Gabriel is coming over and I'm making him dinner. It's our first date."

"Dinner? It's nine o'clock in the evening."

"I don't know, he chose the time. I think he has late afternoon meetings."

"Well, I've been looking him up since you started talking about him and trust me, he has more than enough money to take you out to dinner. Why are you...oh, wait a minute," Mom said, chuckling. "You *are* a Monroe! You *did* get that gene!"

"I'm going now, Mom. I love you, bye!"

"Have fun, sweetie!"

Laughing, I hung up and finished my makeup and got dressed. My dress wasn't perfect, but it was good enough and I still thought I looked fabulous. It showed off just enough cleavage and hid my ass, which was perfect.

As I came downstairs, I found Gabriel sitting in an armchair in the living room, looking at the fireplace. He was in a black suit with a black tie with tiny white dots. When he saw me, he stood up and smiled.

"You look amazing," he said as he walked over and kissed me. "What are you cooking? It smells great."

"Lasagna. It's an old family recipe," I said as I looked around. "I thought you were bringing dessert. Where is it?"

"Don't worry about it, it'll come," he said with a sexy smile. "I'm looking forward to it."

***

After dinner, Gabriel cleared the table and, holding my hand, brought me back into the kitchen. He was still in his suit and I thought about how good he looked both dressed and half naked when he was working out in the gym.

My eyes moved along his tall frame and his wide shoulders, where the fabric on his jacket folded and pulled each time he moved. He had a square jaw and full lips that gave me goose bumps whenever I imagined them on my body. His smile spread across his face and was contagious, but when he wasn't smiling, his blue eyes gave away his thoughts.

His arm went around my waist and he pulled me tight against his strong frame. It amazed me how he could be so strong yet tender at the same time. I was reminded of the chokehold he put on Ryan and smiled.

"What are you thinking about?" he asked.

"Nothing," I said, looking down, trying to hide my grin.

"Want to know what I'm thinking about?"

"Yes."

"Dessert," he said as he raised his eyebrows.

His finger followed the seam of my dress from my shoulder down towards my breasts, and my body shivered in anticipation.

"What's for dessert?" I whispered, barely able to speak.

"You," he said as his eyes locked onto mine. "Do you trust me?"

My lips parted to answer, but I couldn't speak. Gabriel released me and stepped back, moistening his lips.

"Take off your dress," he said.

I slid the dress off my shoulders then let it drop to the floor. Standing in my black lace bra and panties, I was willing to do anything he said.

His eyes soaked in every inch of my body as he removed his suit jacket. His hand reached up to his tie and with a hard tug, he loosened it and pulled it out from under his collar, wrapping it in his hands.

He stepped behind me and held the tie with both of his hands out in front of me. His lips brushed against my ear.

"I'm going to make you come so hard, you'll be begging me to stop," he said. "But I'll just be getting started."

The tie moved closer and Gabriel placed it over my eyes. I reached up to touch it, feeling the silky thread against my fingers as he tied it behind my head. As I lifted an edge, Gabriel moved my hand away.

"Don't touch," he said, sternly.

With the tie so dark, I couldn't see anything so I closed my eyes. I felt on edge but excited, thinking about his words. *Where was he? What was he doing?* I listened and tried to make out what I heard.

The whoosh of the stove lighting. The pantry door opening. The clatter of something as it dropped into a pan. The refrigerator door opening and closing.

Is he cooking?

I started to feel bare so I folded my arms in front of me. Then I felt Gabriel come closer. His lips closed over mine as his hands pulled my arms down. As his lips moved from my lips to my neck, his hand unhooked my bra.

My breath caught as he slipped the straps off my shoulders and the bra dropped to the floor. He pressed me against him and I felt his bare body as he firmly squeezed my butt.

"Relax," he whispered.

He lifted me onto the island and spread my legs as he stepped between them. The granite felt cold against my skin. His warm hands moved over my breasts slowly, roughly, making my nipples harden.

His lips closed over mine again and I pulled him close as his tongue explored my mouth. With his hand behind my head, he leaned me back slowly as he kissed down my neck and my chest until his mouth closed over my nipple.

As I lay down, I felt a towel underneath me, making the counter softer and protecting me from the cold. Gabriel sucked on my nipple while he tugged the other one between his fingers.

He slid his hand down over my hip and thigh then slowly moved it between my legs. As he moved aside my panties, his fingers grazed against my wetness.

With both his hands, he slowly pulled my panties down, leaving me naked on the counter. I held my breath, waiting for his next move as my body throbbed, ready for him.

"Open your mouth," he said.

I opened my mouth, unsure what to expect. A spoon touched my lips and as I tasted melted chocolate, his fingers pressed against my wetness. I gasped as I felt the drizzling of chocolate onto my breasts.

Gabriel's fingers slid over my clit as his mouth slowly licked and sucked the chocolate from my skin. The spoon touched my lips again and as the chocolate entered my mouth, his finger slipped inside of me. I moaned as my hips rocked against his hand. His lips brushed against mine and I sucked his lips, tasting the chocolate.

"It's time," he whispered.

Time?

For a moment he was gone. I didn't feel anything. I didn't hear anything. I wanted to lift the blindfold and peek, but I was afraid he would stop. My body waited for him.

And then he was back. Gabriel's large hands glided up my legs to my hips before pulling me towards him, where he stood between my legs. His hands traveled over my mound then spread my legs more.

His fingers drifted over my pussy before entering me again. As his other hand moved up my stomach, his tongue flicked my swollen clit. I gasped as my body reacted to his every touch.

My head swam from all the sensations. It was too good to be true that my Prince Charming was also good in bed. He clasped his hand firmly onto my hip as his tongue swirled, then his lips brushed against me.

I couldn't take much more. My body pulsed from my core. I grabbed onto the edge of the island as I felt my orgasm approach. Gabriel's tongue moved faster as I reached down and ran my fingers through his hair.

"Oh, I'm close," I said.

I let out a moan, then gasped as he slipped another finger inside of me. A rush swept over my body in waves and my hips bucked. Gabriel kissed the inside of my thigh as his fingers slowed.

My body quivered and I let out a happy sigh. Gabriel's fingers continued and then he moved his thumb over my clit rhythmically from side to side. I laughed from the sensitivity and tried to pull away.

"Stop," I said, giggling.

"Remember what I said before? I'm just getting started."

His fingers thrust deep into me and a moan escaped my lips. My legs felt weak, but my body still responded to his touch. I felt my orgasm rise quicker this time, as if it never had a chance to die away. He knew my body better than I did.

"Oh, please stop," I said, my breaths coming quicker.

The pressure from my core began to build again. I couldn't take it. I had to at least see him, I didn't care what he said before.

I pulled the blindfold off and watched for a moment as Gabriel caressed my body with his free hand. His face looked tender, gentle, but his fingers felt more demanding.

"I can't take it anymore, please, Gabriel, please just fuck me," I cried out.

He smiled and slowed his thrusting fingers, then came over and kissed my lips softly. Without a word, he picked me up and carried me to the thick rug in front of the fireplace.

As he laid me down, he moved between my legs. I reached down and felt his erect manhood and slowly stroked it as he brought it closer to my pussy.

I gasped as he entered me, my body immediately throbbing and pulsing like it had just a moment ago. His movements began slowly, then quickened, hitting deep within me.

Panting, I moved my hands down his muscular back and over his strong ass as it rose and fell with each thrust. He kissed my lips quickly and then whispered in my ear.

"I want you to come again," he said. "I've never seen anything sexier than when you came before."

I couldn't speak, I was too close. My core pulsed as my body moved with his. I began to tremble and then the waves swelled inside of me, traveling throughout my body before crashing over me.

"Oh," I said, the word catching in my throat as my orgasm spread over me.

I opened my eyes and met Gabriel's gaze as he came. His hands moved into my hair, wrapping it around his fists as he held me close to him while his hips rocked slowly.

He kissed me gently and then held me in his arms as my body trembled. I rested my head against his chest as we watched the fire dance. He stood and picked me up, cradling me in his arms.

"Let's go to bed," he said.

***

Gabriel's arms were wrapped around me as I dozed in and out of sleep. His body was solid, muscular, and lean. I pressed myself against him a little more, enjoying the hardness of his body against mine. He squeezed his arms tighter around me and kissed the top of my head.

"Cassie? You awake?" he whispered.

"Yes."

The beep of his alarm went off, startling me. He grabbed his phone and turned it off then looked at me, his eyes a little sad.

"I'm sorry, but I have to go," he said.

"Go? What do you mean?"

He sat up and got out of bed. I wrapped the sheet around myself and followed him downstairs to the kitchen where our clothes still were with the empty condom wrapper on the floor.

"I have an early day tomorrow," he said. "I don't want to wake you."

I had a nagging feeling this had something to do with his unspoken secret. The 'someone else' he mistakenly mentioned. As he pulled his pants on, he turned to face me.

"No, please Cassie. Don't look sad," he said, lifting my chin up to look at him. "I'm sorry. There is nothing more I would love than to spend the night with you, but I just can't right now. Not for a while. I know it's hard for you to understand, but I need to make sure things are right before anything else happens."

"I don't understand," I said, shaking my head.

"I know it doesn't make sense now, but it will soon. I just need you to trust me, okay?"

"I do. I trust you," I said, nodding.

I did trust him, more than I trusted anyone else. But it didn't make his leaving sting any less.

"Are you busy tomorrow? I want to see you again. And the night after that."

"I'll be here," I said. "I want to see you, too."

"Good, I want to spend as much time with you as I can. I need more dessert," he said with a grin.

He put his suit jacket on and put his hand over the inside pocket then smiled.

"I wanted to give you a little something for our first date, but you looked so beautiful I forgot about it," he said as he pulled a small blue box out of his pocket.

"You didn't have to get me anything," I said, putting my hands up.

"Anyone ever tell you you're difficult? I had to force an apartment on you and now I have to force you to take a present," he said, laughing softly.

"Actually, my mother says I'm difficult all the time," I said, laughing.

I took the gift from him and held it in my hand for a moment. The rectangular box was a robin's egg blue with a white bow. Across the box in black lettering was 'Tiffany & Co.'.

While he had given me the watch before, there was something different about this gift now that he was my boyfriend. I wasn't used to getting gifts, especially not of the small box variety, and here he was giving me another small gift.

As I pulled the end of the small white ribbon, I started to get more excited. I couldn't believe Gabriel went out of his way to buy me something. Whatever it was, I knew I would love it.

I set the ribbon on the counter and pulled the lid off the box. Inside the blue box was a hinged box. I opened it and saw glittering diamond drop earrings. My eyes widened and my mouth dropped open. I hadn't expected anything like that.

"I hope you like them," he said.

He took the box from my hand and removed one of the earrings. While I stood there stunned, he put both earrings on me.

"These are too much," I said. "I can't accept this."

"No, they're yours. As soon as I saw them in the store, I knew they were meant for you."

He led me into the powder room and stood behind me as we faced the mirror. My eyes went directly to him, completely dressed in his suit, minus his tie. But his eyes were on me.

My hair was messy from being in bed and my only clothing was the sheet wrapped around me, but the earrings made even that look amazing.

I didn't know what to say. Even though I thought they were too much and I had no idea where or when I would ever wear them, I knew Gabriel wouldn't take no for an answer.

"Thank you," I whispered.

He nodded, looking pleased, then turned me around to face him. His fingers slid my hair behind my ear and then he cupped my face and kissed my lips gently.

"I'll see you tomorrow night," he said. "Late."

Chapter Eleven

Cassie

I sat in my office with my desk calendar open. I couldn't believe how fast time was flying by. Next week it was going to be Christmas Eve and while Gabriel and I had been seeing each other every day, both at work and at the penthouse, neither of us had said anything about the holidays.

Sitting on top of the calendar was my cousin Ashley's home phone number. It had been a few days since I had last spoken to her, and I wondered if she was home.

"Good afternoon, Boone residence," a woman's voice said.

"Hi," I said. "I'm calling for Ashley."

"And whom may I say is calling?"

"Her cousin, Cassie Monroe."

"Please hold."

As I listened to Muzak piped through the phone, I wondered if Gabriel had this kind of set up in his home. Thinking about his home, I felt a twinge of pain in my chest. We had been together for weeks and I had never been to his house.

What's he hiding there?

I stuffed the thought down and reminded myself that I trusted him. He cared about me. There wasn't another woman. *Or was there?* The more I fell for him, the more insecure I felt.

I hated how insecure I felt at times and as a different song came on the hold music, I decided I needed to do something to get my mind off my insecurity. I was ready to hang up when I heard a familiar voice on the line.

"Hey Cassie, I'm sorry you were on hold for so long. I was changing Jacob's diaper."

"It's no problem. I don't think I'll ever get used to calling you and hearing Muzak and everything."

Ashley laughed. "That's Xander for you. He hates silence when he's on hold. How are you doing?"

"I'm good. My mother has been giving me shit about not coming home for Christmas."

"Oh? I guess things are going well between you and Gabriel."

"No, I mean yes." I sighed, feeling frustrated. "I don't know what I mean anymore. Yes, everything seems good, but we just haven't talked about it. I didn't think about it, I just knew I didn't feel like making the trip home."

"Then you have to come over! We're having a party on Christmas Eve, just friends and family. I'd love for you to be there too. And you have to bring Gabriel. As a matter of fact, you don't have to come, I'm more interested in talking to him alone. There's a lot I need to warn him about."

"You are such a bitch," I said, laughing. "I'll ask him. I don't know what he'll say, but I'll ask him."

"You sure you're okay, Cassie? You know I'm here if you want to talk."

"I'm fine, Ash. I just can't believe Christmas is almost here. I'll see you on Christmas Eve."

"Great, I'll see you then!"

As I hung up, I felt bad for lying to my cousin, but I didn't want to get into my insecurities with Gabriel right in the next room. Maybe I was just being selfish wanting more time with him. It had to be just that. I'd feel better if I spent a few minutes with him.

I drummed my fingers on the calendar and looked over to the door that separated my office from Gabriel's. Getting up, I pressed my ear to the door to see if he was on the phone or in a meeting. When I didn't hear anything, I knocked, then opened the door.

"Hey hon," he said as he turned to face the door. "I'm sorry I haven't spent much time with you today. Just a lot of planning going on for the big New Year's Eve fight."

He stood up and wrapped his hands around my waist and kissed my forehead, then my lips. His lips lingered on mine, then slowly pushed my lips open. As his tongue slipped into my mouth, I forgot all about my insecurities.

His phone rang and he looked at the clock and grimaced.

"I'm sorry, Cassie. I'm still matchmaking the undercard. I have to take this call. Is there anything you wanted to talk about? Or can it wait?"

He picked up the phone and pushed the hold button.

"It's okay, it can wait," I said. "But I did want to ask you something. My cousin is having a party Christmas Eve and I was wondering if you'd go with me."

"You want me to meet your family?" he asked.

"Well, I didn't think of it like that, but yes, I do. It would really mean a lot to me if you came."

"Absolutely. I wouldn't miss it," he said, smiling. "But there are a few things I need to do that day. I hate to ask, but is it okay if I meet you there?"

I felt a little disappointed. I didn't like going to parties alone and I imagined showing up at the party on the arm of my suited-up gorgeous prince. But I knew he had a lot on his plate with the big fight, so I smiled and nodded.

"It's okay, as long as we're together."

Chapter Twelve

Cassie

As I sat in the apartment's library in my yoga pants and an oversized t-shirt, I couldn't remember the last time I felt so alone. My mother was right, I should have gone home to see her. I didn't realize that even though I thought it was just another day, it wasn't. It was Christmas Eve.

The doorbell rang and I ran to the door, wondering who it could be. As I looked through the peephole, I recognized Henry, one of the doormen. He was short with thick sandy hair and wrinkles around his eyes. In his hands was a large rectangular box. I opened the door to see what he wanted.

"Hi Henry," I said.

"Good day, Miss Cassie," he said as he entered the apartment and placed the box on the foyer table. "Mr. Kohl delivered this for you and gave me specific instructions."

"He was here? I wonder why he didn't come up."

"He seemed to be in a hurry, Miss."

"Okay, what did he say?"

Henry cleared his throat and pulled out a piece of paper from his lapel pocket and read it.

"Cassie, I bought this for you to wear tonight. Don't be difficult," Henry said.

I laughed, hearing Gabriel's voice in my head.

"Thank you, Henry," I said.

"You're welcome, Miss," he said as he let himself out.

I moved the box to the dining room table. On the top of the box in dark red letters was *Joyeux*, the name of a clothing store I read about recently in a magazine.

After removing the lid, I pushed aside the pink tissue paper and pulled out a black sheath dress with a plunging V on the back. I held it up against me and thought it would fit. Underneath the dress was a glittery clutch.

I couldn't fight with Gabriel about it. He wasn't even there. And for the first time, I didn't want to fight. As I looked at the dress in front of me, I realized I never thought about what I was wearing to Ashley's party that night.

As I put the dress back into the box, a card slid onto the floor. I picked it up, recognizing Gabriel's handwriting.

Wear the earrings.
Love, Gabriel

Smiling, I carried the dress upstairs. It was time to get ready. I couldn't wait to see Ashley after all this time and to spend the evening with Gabriel.

***

I was dressed and ready to go to Jefferson Manor, Ashley's home, but I couldn't shake my loneliness. *Where was Gabriel? What was he doing?* I was driving myself crazy with questions I couldn't answer.

Calling down to the lobby, I recognized Henry's voice when he answered the phone.

"What can I do for you, Miss?" he asked.

"Can you call a cab for me?"

"Mr. Kohl's driver is here waiting for you."

Stan was standing beside the limo when I stepped outside. He smiled and nodded at me, then opened the back door.

"By myself? Can't I ride in front with you?" I asked.

"Mr. Kohl instructed me--"

"Say no more, I got it, Stan," I said as I climbed into the back.

Alone in the back of the limo, I didn't feel any better. I fidgeted in the seat and couldn't even distract myself with the passing scenery. If it hadn't been for Ashley, I would have said I had a headache or something and stayed at home.

The limo shook as it went over the gravel driveway leading up to Jefferson Manor. Stan lowered the divider and looked at me through his mirror.

"We're almost there. It's just up ahead," he said.

"Do you know when Gabriel will be here?" I asked.

Stan's eyes darted away and I leaned forward to try to catch him again in the mirror. As I widened my eyes at him, he let out a small sigh.

"I don't know. He's otherwise engaged at the moment," he said.

"What the hell does that mean?"

"He forbade me to say. Please don't make this more difficult for me."

"Difficult for you? Are you kidding me?"

"He will be here later, but I don't know when," he said as he raised the divider.

The limo stopped in front of the Georgian mansion, but I was so inside my head that I barely noticed anything other than the oversized wreath on the door. I rang the doorbell as I watched Stan drive away.

"Cassie! I'm so glad you came," Ashley said.

Ashley had on a green dress with sparkling trim and a Santa hat. She threw her arms around me and we hugged each other tightly.

"It's always good to see you," I said.

"Where's your man? I thought Gabriel was coming with you."

"I don't know," I said with a sigh. "He said he'd meet me here."

"Come with me. I know that look, but we're adults now, which means you need a drink."

I followed Ashley past a curved stairway and into the kitchen. Several people dressed in chef attire were cooking. We walked towards the back where there was a small table and chairs set up. I recognized Tara right away as she poured rum into a punch bowl.

"I think that should do it," she said with her thick Southern drawl.

"Tara makes a really lethal eggnog," Ashley said as Tara handed me a cup.

"Let me know what you think," Tara said. "It's an old family recipe of 'add enough rum until you can't see straight.'"

"Sounds perfect," I said.

"Sit," Ashley said as she sat at the table. "What's going on?"

I sighed. The last thing I wanted to do was start whining at a Christmas party. But as I looked across the table at Ashley, I knew I needed to get it all off my chest.

"I'm just confused, that's all. I mean he comes over late, he never stays the night, I've never even been to his house. I don't even know where he lives," I said. "I know you said to listen to my gut, but that stupid thing doesn't know what's going on. One second it tells me to trust him and the next, I just don't know anymore."

"What do you think is going on with him?" she asked.

"Gabriel's in love with someone else," I said. "I'm sure of it."

"How do you know?" Ashley asked.

"Did you see him with her?" Tara asked.

"No, I didn't. I just know he is. Why else isn't he here? He said he'd meet me, which I thought was strange, but whatever. But now he's going to be late. I trust him, but right now I'm having a hard time doing that."

I took a sip of the eggnog and shivered from its strength. I felt a strange vibration under my hands and my brow wrinkled as I tried to figure out what it was until I realized it was the phone in my bag that I had placed on the table.

Shaking my head, I thought about how stupid this ridiculousness with Gabriel made me. If I trusted him and didn't think too much, everything was fine. But once I started to piece together all the other things, I remembered what Mack said on my first day about Gabriel.

That man is in deep with someone else.

Taking my phone out of my bag, I saw Gabriel's name flash across the screen. I got up and moved to a quieter spot in the kitchen and answered.

"Hello?" I said, fighting the urge to answer with 'what now?'

"I'm sorry, Cassie," Gabriel said. "This isn't how I wanted Christmas Eve to turn out."

"Yeah well, it is what it is," I said angrily.

"We need to talk. Ask your cousin if there's somewhere private you and I can meet."

I handed the phone to Ashley.

"You talk to him," I said. "I'm not in the mood for this."

Ashley took the phone and I heard her voice as she spoke to him, but I was too preoccupied to listen. After a few minutes, she handed the phone back to me.

"He's going to meet you in the gazebo in the rose garden," she said. "He made me promise you'd be there, he said it's really important. You can borrow my coat if you need to."

"No, I'll be fine," I said. "Just show me where to go."

I couldn't help but feel like I was walking to my death. *We need to talk.* How many times had he said that to me? Nothing good ever came from that phrase.

As Ashley and I went out the front door, she hooked her arm through mine.

"Whatever happens tonight, you have to come back," Ashley said. "We need to spend some time together, just you and me."

"We do," I said. "And thanks for listening to me. Things have been crazy lately and I guess I'm just confused. I haven't told him yet, but...I love him and I think it's making me crazy."

"I've been there," she said with a smile. "But one thing, Cassie. I know I don't know him, but just from talking to him on the phone, I could tell he really does care about you. I know you, so don't take this the wrong way, but just shut up and listen to him, okay?"

"Okay, okay, I promise," I said.

Tiny white lights lit the rose garden, making it look dreamy. Ashley gave me a hug and walked back to the house as I followed the path to the center where the gazebo stood. Gabriel stood in the middle in a black suit with a red tie. In his hands was a large bouquet of red roses. As I entered the gazebo, he smiled.

"These are for you," he said as he handed me the flowers.

"Thank you, they're beautiful," I said. "But you're still late."

"I know you're angry, but you try finding two dozen red roses on Christmas Eve," he said with a smile. "I'm sorry I'm late, but I promise it'll never happen again."

I nodded and sat down. There was so much on my mind that I had to get out. I needed to say what I was thinking and then, as I promised Ashley, I would shut up.

"Gabriel, I trust you, I really do, but I can't keep going like this. There's too much I can't ignore anymore."

"I know, Cassie," he said, taking my hands in his as he sat beside me. "And that's what we need to talk about. I have to tell you something."

He looked down for a moment before his eyes came up and met mine. I felt foolish for being so angry and insecure before. His eyes told me everything I needed to know. It was why I trusted him in the first place.

"You can tell me anything," I said. "You know that."

"I know. And I'm sure I know how you'll react, but what if I'm wrong? I don't want to make any mistakes, especially not with you. So I waited to make sure things were right between us."

I was sitting on the edge of my seat, waiting to hear what was bothering him, what was so huge that he couldn't tell me until now. There were so many things I wanted to say, but I had promised to shut up so I was doing exactly that.

"Okay, I'm listening," I said as I bit my tongue.

"I love you, Cassie. I know I haven't said it before, but I've been in love with you for a while now."

For a moment I was speechless, but then the words flew out of my mouth.

"I love you too, Gabriel," I said, unable to stop myself from smiling. "Now please, tell me what's going on. You're making me nervous."

"I know you think there's someone else in my life, and it's true, there is, but not like you think. I have a daughter."

The tenderness in his eyes when he spoke about his daughter was enough to make me understand his feelings for her. He *was* in deep with someone else, his child. How could I not admire that?

All my insecurity and anger was for nothing and as quickly as it had escalated, it vanished just as fast. Hearing those four words, everything suddenly made sense.

"Why didn't you tell me? Is she here? What's her name? How old is she? I have so many questions," I said excitedly. "I want to meet her."

"Slow down," he said, laughing. "Wendy's inside with Ashley. She's been dying to meet you."

"Really? You told her about me?"

"Of course I did," he said. "It was important to me that she knew what was going on and that she was okay with it. She's only nine, but she's mature for her age."

"But wait, were you married? Are you married? What about her mother?"

"No, no, Dakota and I grew up together. She had been through a lot and I was her crutch. She didn't have anywhere to go so when she told me she was pregnant, I moved her into my apartment, a dive near the old gym. It didn't matter that the baby wasn't mine, I loved Dakota and wanted to take care of her. I couldn't love Wendy more if she was my own flesh and blood."

"But then how is Wendy your daughter?"

"Dakota is a free spirit," he said. "She can't stay in one place for very long and she knew it was bad for a child. I wanted to make sure Wendy got the best of everything, so I built the MMAC from the ground up. Then four years ago when Dakota asked me to adopt Wendy, I didn't even hesitate. I said yes. I changed my life for her. So when I met you, it was important that she was okay with me dating."

Everything with Gabriel had happened so quickly, but for the first time, it all fell into place for me. I realized that even though things had happened so fast, one thing remained clear -- I was in love with Gabriel, and learning about Wendy didn't change that. If anything, it made me love him more, the way he could take care of a child that was not his own showed me just how much love he had to give.

"Then let's go inside," I said, standing. "I can't wait to meet her."

Gabriel took my hand and we followed the path back to the house. When we came inside, Ashley was waiting by the door.

"Well?" she asked. "Everything okay?"

"I can't believe you didn't tell me," I said, hugging her.

"Wendy is in the living room playing with the other kids," Ashley said as she pointed to the room ahead of us.

As Gabriel and I entered the room, a pretty young girl with her long black hair in a headband stood up. She was wearing a red dress with white faux fur around the collar, cuffs, and hem. Her smile lit up her face and she rushed over and gave Gabriel a hug before turning to me.

"You must be Cassie," she said. "I'm Wendy. Did you like the roses? I told him he had to bring you flowers."

"Thank you, Wendy, that was very thoughtful of you. They're beautiful. Did you pick them?"

"I helped, but he's a little stubborn and doesn't take my advice often," she said with a shrug.

"She definitely knows you," I said to Gabriel.

"I've been wanting to meet you for a while, but Daddy thought we should wait. I kept telling him to invite you to dinner."

"Wait a second," I said. "Dinner? So you'd eat dinner with Wendy and then have dinner with me?"

"Why do you think I spend so much time working out? I had a lot of calories to burn off," Gabriel said, laughing. "What can I say? It made sense at the time."

"I think Wendy and I have a lot of talking to do," I said.

"You wouldn't believe the things I could tell you," she said, grinning.

Ashley's toddler son, Jacob, came up and tugged at Wendy's dress then grabbed her hand. As they walked away, Gabriel wrapped his arms around my waist and pulled me close.

"Wendy and I discussed this earlier, and we'd love it if you stayed the night and spent Christmas with us," he said.

I didn't know what came over me, but my eyes misted over and I had to blink back tears. I couldn't imagine anything more perfect than spending Christmas with Gabriel and his daughter. I hoped it would be the first of many mornings together.

***

By the end of the evening, Wendy was sitting on the couch looking sleepy. My old insecurities crept up again as I watched her lay her head on the arm of the couch. She seemed to be excited to meet me earlier, but what if she didn't mean it?

"Hi Wendy," I said, sitting beside her.

"Hi," she said with a yawn. "Are you sleeping over tonight?"

"Yes, if that's okay with you. You can tell me if it's weird or you don't want me to. I'll understand."

"I don't mind," she said with a shrug. "You seem nice. Dakota always had all kinds of people around and never asked me what I thought. I mean Mom."

I couldn't help but wonder if deep down she was hoping her parents would end up together. Before I could stop myself, the words spilled out of my big mouth.

"Did you ever wish your parents would get together?"

Wendy cracked a big smile. "You're funny," she said, then shook her head. "I never really thought about it before. I don't even remember them living together when I was little. Mom drives Daddy crazy, and I think it's better that they're not together. I've never seen him smile at her like he does at you."

Really? I wanted to ask, but I couldn't. That was crossing the line. *But maybe another time.*

"Where's Dad? I want to go home," she said, yawning again.

I looked around the room and noticed Gabriel by a tall window talking to a man with longer dark hair and a closely cropped beard. I didn't need an introduction to know that it was Xander Boone, Ashley's husband. But as much as I wanted to meet him, I knew Wendy needed to get home to bed.

Gabriel looked towards us and smiled, then his face filled with concern as he watched Wendy drop her head onto the arm of the sofa. He shook Xander's hand and came over to us.

"Let's go home," he said. "Tomorrow's a big day."

Chapter Thirteen

Cassie

We rode in the back of the limo in silence while Wendy slept, her head resting on Gabriel's lap. For once, I had nothing to say and it made me glad. Gabriel twined his fingers with mine as we held hands and whenever I looked up at him, his eyes told me what I wanted to know--he really did love me.

Looking into the darkness, I felt the sway of the road as we climbed up a hill. It was an area of Canyon Cove I had never been to before. On each hillcrest were massive estate homes with soft golden lights illuminating them. Despite my mother reminding me of the wealth in Canyon Cove, it wasn't until that moment that I realized she wasn't exaggerating.

You know what they say, you can't turn around in Canyon Cove without bumping into a billionaire.

I laughed, hearing my mother's words in my head. Gabriel tilted his head and his dark hair fell onto his forehead. His brow wrinkled and his eyes scrunched before he leaned towards me.

"What's so funny?" he whispered.

"Nothing," I said. "Just thinking about something my mother told me."

Luckily, he let it drop and I went back to gazing into the darkness. The limo turned onto a narrow road then stopped. Even though it didn't matter to me if Gabriel lived in a box at the side of the road, I was still curious to see his home. I was probably even more curious after living in his penthouse apartment all this time.

Ahead of us was a large iron gate that slowly began to open. Other than the trees lining the driveway, I couldn't see much else. I tried to look ahead, through Stan's windshield, but his headlights didn't reveal anything.

The car drove on for what felt like forever before curving in front of the house. And I was happy to see that it was a house. Despite how large it was, it was homey in comparison to the mansions I saw earlier.

Gabriel's mansion was a grey stone colonial with a circular portico at the front door. The tall windows were accented with off-white window casing that stood out from the stone. The wooden double door had glass panes with wrought iron bars covering them. Hanging from the portico was a bronze lantern-styled lamp.

I had never seen a house like this before and as I turned to look at Gabriel, I wondered how he went from a fighter who worked out at that old gym by my apartment to the man who lived here.

As Stan stopped the car in front of the house, Wendy's head popped up. Her face was groggy as she looked out the window then opened the car door. Gabriel stepped out behind her, then held my hand as I exited the limo.

I followed Wendy into the house as Stan handed Gabriel a shopping bag with *Joyeux* across the middle. The entry hall was wide with a curving staircase on one side and a swirling wrought iron rail across the balcony above. The floors were white marble and black inlaid squares and the walls were a soft white color. Hanging in the center was an antique bronze and crystal chandelier. Wendy went directly to the curved staircase and began to head upstairs.

"I'll be right up, Wendy," Gabriel said, his voice echoing.

He put his arm around me and led me through the open double doors leading to the back of the house. Grabbing a remote, he turned on the fireplace at one end of the room, then lit the tall Christmas tree at the other end. The room had thick beige carpeting and light cocoa-colored walls. A large couch faced the fireplace and above it hung a TV. While the room was large, it felt warm and homey.

"Make yourself at home," he said. "There's a bar to the left with soda and juice. Down the hall is the kitchen. The bag is for you. I'll be back in a few minutes."

He kissed the top of my head before leaving me alone. I was too overwhelmed to do anything but stand there for a moment. Never in a million years did I ever think I would be standing in a mansion. And despite my mother's jokes, I certainly never thought of my boyfriend as a billionaire.

I pushed it all out of my head. I couldn't let this place overwhelm me or make me feel out of place. I wouldn't allow that. Especially not when I was spending the night with Gabriel for the first time. This night, meeting Wendy and knowing I would be sleeping in Gabriel's arms, was special, and that was all that mattered to me.

In front of me was the *Joyeux* bag. I picked it up and carried it to the plush couch and sat down. After kicking off my shoes, I tucked my feet underneath me and peeked into the bag. It was full of clothes.

One by one I pulled out each item. A cotton pajama set with cherries on it was followed by a silky red sleepshirt with white trim. After that was lacy lingerie in several colors, then a pair of jeans, a dark purple sweater, and even black yoga pants and a purple sweatshirt similar to my favorite ones at home.

"I had to guess your size," Gabriel said as he entered the room again. "But I knew if you said yes, you wouldn't have anything to wear tomorrow."

"Thank you, but you didn't have to do this."

"It's what I do, Cassie. I take care of the people close to me."

He removed his suit jacket and sat beside me before pressing a button on the remote. Soft music filled the room. His arm slipped behind my shoulders. Gently, he touched my cheek as he lowered his head towards mine. I tilted my head up, waiting for his kiss.

"What were you laughing about before?" he asked.

My eyes flew open and met Gabriel's blue eyes. With a wide grin, he raised his eyebrow up and I laughed.

"I told you before, nothing."

"I heard you say nothing, but you also said it was something your mother said. With the few things you've mentioned about her, I know it has to be something good. Spill it."

"No, trust me, it's really not something you need to hear. You won't find it funny anyway."

"Try me," he said.

I pursed my lips as I thought about it. As I played her words in my head again, I shook my head.

"No way," I said. "Just no. It's too embarrassing."

"It was something about the wealth here, wasn't it? Maybe a joke about you finding a billionaire or something. Am I right?"

I nodded, unable to read his face. "But it's like you said, she's a funny woman."

"I didn't come from this," he said. "Sometimes I look around and it seems foreign to me that I even live here."

He loosened his tie and unbuttoned the first couple of buttons on his shirt.

"Then how did all of this happen?"

"Because of Wendy," he said, smiling softly. "We moved around a lot when I was growing up. My mother couldn't seem to settle in one place, the grass was always greener somewhere else."

Gabriel was quiet. His jaw tightened and his eyes narrowed as he stared into the room. A vein throbbed at his temple. I leaned forward, trying to catch his eye, but he wasn't there.

"Gabriel? Are you okay?"

He shook his head and turned back towards me, his eyes sad.

"I was just thinking about Dakota and how much she's like my mother. After Dakota moved in, I tried my best for us to be a family. My brother

Gideon was also living with us, and I supported us all by fighting. I dropped out of college so I could spend my days training, and at night I took any and every fight I could get. I didn't care if they were legal fights or street fights, I just needed to make money."

"Why was your brother living with you? What happened to your mother?"

"I don't know what happened to her. It's hard for me to wrap my mind around it. I mean things weren't great when I was a kid, but I always thought we were happy. But sometime after Gideon turned two, things started to change. Eventually she was never there for us. Once I was thirteen, my brother and I were pretty much on our own."

"Where's Gideon now?"

"I guess he's out. He should have been here by now. He's a student at Canyon Cove University, but he stays here during breaks. He's been having a hard time at school and sometimes I have to convince him to stay, but he's really smart and very talented and I think he can really make something of himself. He seems to think what I did was easy though, and he figures he can do the same."

"So what *did* you do? How did you go from fighting to this?"

"After Wendy was born, something clicked in me. I wanted to make sure she never wanted for anything in her life. I heard some guys were making money from booking fights, so I got involved with that while I was still fighting. The money was good, but after Dakota and Wendy left, I started filling my time with other things."

Other things. I know what that means. Mack warned me about those other things.

"Did you know Mack back then?" I asked.

He laughed as he nodded. "Yes, he saw probably a lot more than I realized at the time. What can I say? The ladies love me," he said with a sly grin.

"The ladies love you," I said, rolling my eyes. "You are such a jerk sometimes."

"But you love me anyway, right?"

"Maybe."

I tried to hold back my smile, but the way he was looking at me with that grin and the playful look in his eyes, I couldn't help myself. He lifted my hand and brought it up to his lips before closing his other hand on top of it.

"Once I started booking fights, I figured out a way to incentivize trainers to work with me more so I could arrange some really great fights. Since Mack had some of the best fighters around, I reached out to him. Eventually I got to the point where I was making enough money to have these trainers and fighters book fights only through me. That's when the MMAC was born."

"That's really amazing. You make it sound so simple."

"At times it felt that way, but I got lucky," he said. "If I started it a year later, the MMAC wouldn't have become what it is today. The timing was perfect, and that was all because of Wendy. I would have never been more than just a fighter if it wasn't for her. I try to keep most of our fights here in Canyon Cove so I can attend."

"Does Mack know about Wendy?"

"No, I've kept her completely out of the business. I don't want anything interfering with Wendy's life. She's had enough to deal with. So when Dakota asked if I would take custody of her, the first thing I did was find a house where she could just be a kid and not have to worry about anyone knocking on the door at all hours of the night."

"Mmm-hmm, the other things," I said.

"Don't be jealous, that was way before I met you. You're the only 'other thing' for me now."

He slid his arms around me and pulled me closer. I rested my head against his chest as he stroked my hair. A door slammed shut and the thump of boots came down the hall. A man in his early twenties in jeans and a faded green t-shirt walked into the room. He was around Gabriel's height and had a similar strong jaw, but was lanky, with tousled sandy blond hair. In his hands were several wrapped gifts.

"I hope I'm not interrupting," he said. "I brought Santa's gifts in from the hiding place." He put the gifts under the tree, then held his hand out to me. "I'm Gideon, the good looking one in the family."

"It's nice to meet you," I said, shaking his hand. "I'm Cassie."

"Well hello, Cassie," Gideon said as he sat down beside me. "You should let me draw you some time."

"Let me guess, like one of your French girls," I said.

"How did you know?" he said with a wink.

"That's enough, Gideon. I thought you were in love with…"

"Yeah, well she started to get clingy so I had to end that. But I promise I'll let you have Cassie. Consider it your Christmas gift from me," Gideon said.

"You wish you could get me," I said.

"You're right, I do," Gideon said, grinning. "Do you have a sister?"

As I laughed, I tried to hide a yawn. It wasn't that late, but with everything that had happened, I suddenly felt tired.

"I'm sure Wendy will be up early," Gabriel said. "I'll show you to your room."

Gabriel picked up the shopping bag and we went upstairs. After all the ups and downs of the day, I was too tired to pay attention to anything. He opened the door to a bedroom and turned on the lights.

"Wendy's room is next door and I'm at the end of the hall," he said. "I had the bathroom stocked with everything imaginable."

I felt a pang of disappointment that we weren't going to be sleeping in each other's arms after all, but it quickly disappeared. With Wendy in the next room, I wouldn't feel right about it anyway. I peeked into the adjoining bathroom and noticed an oversized tub.

"Ooh, that looks nice," I said. "A bubble bath would be perfect right now."

"I wish I could join you," he said as he kissed my forehead and held me close. "Good night, Cassie. And Merry Christmas."

"Good night."

Gabriel closed the door behind him. As the tub filled with warm water, I opened a closet door and found shelves of every kind of bubble bath, soap, and bath salts I could imagine.

Wow, he wasn't kidding, I thought.

I poured in a capful of a cucumber and white tea bubble bath and watched the bubbles grow. As I got into the tub, I noticed a button near the tap. Pressing the button started jets in the tub that I hadn't noticed before. I positioned my back against one of the jets and leaned back, letting the aroma and relaxation of the bath take over me as I closed my eyes.

Chapter Fourteen

Gabriel

I got up early on Christmas Day, grateful to have the people I loved all under my roof. The sun hadn't risen yet, but that was normal for me. Since my fighting days, I always woke before dawn.

Quietly rolling off the bed, I pulled on a pair of jeans and a t-shirt. I didn't sleep well. I couldn't. Not after what Wendy told me before she fell asleep. I needed to take a walk and clear my head.

Christmas Eve

"Make yourself at home," I said. "There's a bar to the left with soda and juice. Down the hall is the kitchen. The bag is for you. I'll be back in a few minutes."

I felt bad leaving Cassie alone, but I wanted to say good night to Wendy and make sure she was okay with Cassie.

Entering Wendy's bedroom, I picked up a stuffed bear that was lying on the floor as I made my way towards her. She looked sweet with her hair spread out on the pillow in her pajamas. Her eyes were heavy but she wiggled her fingers at me.

"I wanted to talk to you before you fell asleep," I said.

As I sat on the edge of her bed, I pressed the bear's nose against her cheek, and she giggled then hugged the bear tight as she sat up.

"Sure," she said with a yawn. "What do you want to talk about?"

"Tonight and Cassie. I want to make sure you're okay with everything."

"Yeah, Dad, I really like her. I would've told you if I didn't."

I laughed. "You're right, you're right. I know you would have."

"I really do like her, Dad. She seems nice and I liked talking to her. But as long as she makes you happy, that's what matters."

"You really are mature for your age, you know that?"

She nodded. "Wise beyond my years," she said. "There is something I've been wanting to talk to you about though."

Her big dark eyes darted away from me and she held the bear up higher as if she was hiding.

"What is it?" I asked.

"You know Dakota is going to call tomorrow," she said before hesitating. "There's something I was supposed to ask you, but I didn't."

"What is it?"

"The last time she called…remember when Karen freaked out?"

"Did something happen? Don't tell me I fired her for no reason," I said.

"Well, no, she really was kinda crazy. But she overheard me on the phone with Mom and I think she might have gotten the wrong idea."

"What did she hear?"

"Mom said she got a place of her own in Arizona and she's ready to settle down."

Hearing the words knocked the wind out of me. I tried to keep my face from showing how upset I was, but I couldn't.

"She wants you back," I said, trying to hide the disbelief and anger from my voice.

"No," Wendy said, giggling. "She just wants me to visit."

I sighed with relief. It didn't matter to me that Dakota was Wendy's biological mother, I would fight her tooth and nail for Wendy if it ever came to that.

"Do you want to go?"

"I wasn't sure," she said. "That's why it took me so long to tell you. But I think it might be okay. She said there's a lot of things to do. And she wants to spend time with me."

"I hate the thought of you being away, but if it's what you want, then okay. Did she say when?"

"No, she said she would talk to you about it."

Wendy looked down at the bed and I could see there was more she wasn't saying.

"Are you sure you're okay?"

"My friends at school all do things with their moms. I sometimes feel left out because I don't have one."

"You have a mom."

"I know I do, but you know what I mean," she said. "She's never around. She hasn't invited me to visit since I moved here. Maybe it'll be different this time."

"I'm sure it will be," I lied. "I'll talk to her tomorrow, sweetie. Now go to sleep. You know Santa won't come unless you're asleep."

"Ha, yeah right, Dad. Santa," she said.

She laid back down and I kissed her cheek before pulling the covers up to her chin. Wendy pushed the covers down and rolled over onto her side with her bear in her arms.

As I walked out of her bedroom, my mind was on Dakota. I had to have faith that she would do the right thing and take care of Wendy. But I hated the thought of leaving her there.

Christmas Day

The walk made me feel better, but I still dreaded talking to Dakota. I couldn't stop Wendy from seeing her mother though, not if it was something she really wanted to do.

Entering the house, a strange but familiar scent hit me. *Pancakes?* I made my way into the kitchen. Standing at the stove was Cassie in the yoga pants and sweatshirt I bought for her. She smiled at me as she flipped pancakes like a pro. Behind her, Wendy was busy setting the table.

"What's going on here?" I asked.

"There's the old man," Gideon said as he exited the pantry with a jug of syrup. "Cassie said we had to have pancakes on Christmas morning. I wasn't going to complain."

"She even made me tree-shaped pancakes," Wendy said, holding up her plate.

I slipped my hand around Cassie's waist and kissed her temple as she flipped another pancake.

"You didn't have to do this," I whispered.

"Yes, I did," she said, handing me a plate with a stack of pancakes on it. "You kind of took me by surprise inviting me at the last minute. I don't have gifts for any of you, so right now I'm making breakfast. Later, Wendy said she wants to bake Christmas cookies--"

"Cassie said she has a secret recipe for chocolate chip cookies," Wendy said.

"That's right, I do," Cassie said. "And Gideon told me you always keep a stocked kitchen, so I'll whip something up later for dinner. It's the least I can do."

"Can we keep her?" Gideon said as he stuffed a piece of pancake in his mouth. "And seriously, please tell me you have a sister."

The phone rang and I knew it was Dakota. As Cassie sat down with Wendy and Gideon, I thought about letting the call go to voicemail. But if I did that, I might never get a hold of Dakota. She was impossible to reach.

"I'm sorry, it's probably Dakota," I said. "Go ahead and start without me." As I carried the phone out of the kitchen, I hit the button to answer. "Kohl residence."

"I always think it's funny that you still answer your own phone," Dakota said.

"I might have a lot, but I don't want to warp Wendy's perspective of how life is."

"Like I have?"

"I didn't say that," I said.

"You didn't have to, Gabriel. But that's the thing, just as you changed, so have I. I want to see her. I want to spend time with my daughter."

"You can always come here to visit. You know you're welcome to stay anytime."

"I have my own home now. Things are different. I met someone and he lives here. I want to settle down."

"And what about Wendy?"

Dakota was silent for a moment. "I don't know."

"What does that mean?" I asked, trying to rein in my anger.

"Listen, I know you can provide for her and give her whatever she wants. You've given her the only stability she's known in her life. But I don't know. Maybe she should live with me now."

"Over my dead body," I said. "You want her to visit you, that's fine. But that's it, Dakota. Visits. Nothing more."

"We'll discuss this after she visits me. I think the decision should be left to her."

"Fine, that's the smartest thing you've ever said."

"When can I see her?"

Entering my office, I flipped on the light and walked over to my desk. I flipped my desk calendar towards me. If I had to let Wendy visit Dakota, I would make sure I wasn't very far.

"Wendy said you're in Arizona. How far are you from Phoenix?"

"About an hour," she said.

"How about February? President's Day weekend."

"A weekend? I really think during the week would be better."

"She's not taking off from school."

"Oh right, school," she said, sounding disappointed. "Alright then, whenever, that's fine."

"We'll firm up the details another time. I'll get Wendy."

"No, it's alright. I'm actually in a bit of a rush. Let her know I'll call to talk to her another time."

Just as I was about to blow up at Dakota over not talking to her daughter on Christmas day, she hung up. My temper flared and I clenched my fists, looking for the nearest thing to hit. It reminded me of why I became a fighter to begin with.

I stepped outside into the cool air and took a few breaths. How dare Dakota do this on Christmas and then not talk to her own daughter? I didn't know what I was going to say to Wendy, but

I knew it didn't matter. She knew her mother well enough. Just like I knew my own.

Entering the house again, I thought about how I had been surrounded by Dakotas my entire life. It was the reason I kept Wendy a secret from Cassie for so long. It was hard for me to understand that someone like Cassie existed. I didn't want to admit it to myself, but I sometimes thought Cassie might be too good to be true.

As I walked back to the kitchen, I stood back as I watched Cassie and Wendy talking. It was surreal to have them together, but it was time. I really should have done it sooner. The way I felt about Cassie, I wanted to move things forward. While I had been worried she wouldn't accept my having a daughter, I now knew that was foolish. It was just another excuse of mine, a way I protected myself.

I had to push all the drama aside and remember that today was Christmas. I would avoid telling Wendy about Dakota for as long as I could.

"Was that Mom?" Wendy asked.

"Yes, but—"

"It's okay, you don't have to make anything up," she said. "She's always busy."

Wendy turned back to Cassie and they continued their conversation. I was glad Wendy wasn't upset about not talking to her mother. And as I sat down at the table across from Wendy and Cassie, they both smiled at me and I knew everything would be alright.

Chapter Fifteen

Cassie

Ryan was in my office, finishing the last of his shoulder stretches, when I noticed it was almost three o'clock.

"How's that feel?" I asked. "I think you've been showing a lot of improvement. You should be able to take that fight next month."

"I sure hope. I have friends in Phoenix. It would be awesome to have them there supporting me. You're going to be there too, right?"

"Yes, I will."

"Good, I know I was a dick when you first started a few months ago, but you're really my good luck charm. I don't think Mack would've kept me if it wasn't for you."

"You're a good fighter, Ryan," I said as I looked at my watch. "I don't mean to kick you out, but--"

"Nah, it's fine. I've been here too long already. I need to hit the shower."

As Ryan left my office, Gabriel appeared in the doorway. Gabriel kept an eye on him until he was out of view, then smiled as he walked in.

"I know you say he's a good kid, but I still don't trust him being alone with you," he said.

"I think you're jealous," I teased.

"Well, I haven't had a lot of time alone with you lately," he said as he pulled me close. "Seems like all I get are these few minutes again."

"I'm sorry, but Wendy's really excited about her trip and has a list of things she wants to get."

"I know she is. And she already told me it's not cool to go shopping with me. I think she likes you better than me anyway."

I laughed. "You know that's not true. Wendy is a huge daddy's girl."

"I know. I guess I'm just worried about losing her. I don't trust Dakota. And Wendy is putting so much into this trip. I'm worried she's going to be really disappointed."

"It's only a long weekend. I'm sure everything will be okay."

"I have to go pick her up at school now," he said. "You sure you don't want to come? I promise I won't tell your boss you left early."

"No, go. Spend some time with Wendy. I need to clean up here and take care of a few things anyway."

"I love you," he said as he bent down to kiss my lips.

"I love you too."

"Gah, it's enough to make me sick," Mack said as he entered my office.

"I love you too, Mack," Gabriel said, patting Mack on the back as he left.

Mack grumbled at Gabriel as he made himself comfortable in one of the chairs. Once Gabriel was gone, Mack raised an eyebrow at me and cocked his head towards the door.

"Shut the door," he said.

I closed the door and sat down across from Mack.

"Something wrong?" I asked.

"Did you hear what the suit did?"

My mind spun as I tried to figure out what he was talking about but came up blank.

"What are you talking about? The February fight?"

"Nah, not that. I mean I'm glad you'll be there, but that's not what I'm talking about. Have you spoken to Becca?"

"Last week sometime. Why? Did Gabriel do something to her?"

"Not just to her. I'll let her tell you what loverboy did. It's bullshit if you ask me. He's playing with people's feelings and messing with their minds."

Mack grunted as he stood and grumbled all the way out of my office. I had no idea what he was talking about, and I wondered why Becca hadn't called me if something as bad as Mack made it seem had happened.

I called Becca's work number, knowing she usually answered the phones. The phone rang more than she usually let it and when it was answered, it was an unfamiliar voice on the other end.

"Housing."

"Hi, I'm calling for Rebecca Draven," I said.

"No, sorry, she doesn't work here anymore."

My stomach sank as I hung up the phone. *If Gabriel did something to make her lose her job, she could be mad at me.* It was the only reason I could think of for why Becca wouldn't have told me.

For a moment I thought about calling Gabriel and yelling at him, but I couldn't believe he would do something that would make Becca lose her job. *What did he have to do with her job anyway?* I pulled my cell phone out of my purse and tapped on Becca's name.

"Hello?" Becca said.

The background was noisy like if she was at a party. I wondered if she took another restaurant job to make ends meet. I was still paying my old rent to help Becca out these past few months that I had been living at Gabriel's penthouse, but maybe it wasn't enough anymore.

I felt bad that I left her in that crummy apartment and somehow cost her her job. I tried to think of what to say, but anything I thought of made me feel worse. *Move in with me. Maybe I can get you a job here. I can lend you some money.* She'd never let me help her like that anyway. She hated that I was still sending her rent.

"Hello? Cassie?"

"I'm so sorry, Becca," I finally blurted out.

"Wait a second, it's too noisy here," she said. I heard a door close and then Becca's voice returned. "Okay, that's better. I feel like such a bad friend, but things happened so fast I haven't had much time to myself."

"I'm sorry," I said, unable to say anything else.

"Hey, I'm getting out of here in a few minutes. Meet me at Mirabella's."

"Mirabella's? What time? Are you taking the bus?"

"No, I'll walk. It's just a couple blocks from here."

"A couple of blocks? Where are you?"

"City Hall. Can you skip out early? Meet me in fifteen."

"Okay, I'll be there," I said.

***

It was late afternoon, too early for the dinner crowd, and Mirabella's Café was dead. I was glad I opted for pants this morning instead of a skirt. I would have frozen my butt off with the cold wind that whipped past me on my walk.

Becca was already there, sitting at a four top table in a corner. She was dressed in a dark tan pantsuit I had never seen before and her light brown hair was down instead of in the ponytail she usually wore at the restaurant. She smiled widely as I sat down and looked giddy. I was totally confused.

"I'm so happy to see you," she said. "You know when you first started telling me about Gabriel, I really thought he was just some spoiled ass with a lot of money. But I was wrong."

"You never told me you thought that."

"I know I didn't. I'll be honest, I kept waiting for him to make a mistake, especially after that Monica neighbor of yours showed up right after you moved in. But he didn't and now because of you, things are going to be amazing. I owe you so much, Cassie."

"What are you talking about? I thought you lost your job."

"Lost my job? No, why would you think that?"

"I was talking to Mack and he seemed pretty upset. I called you at work and the woman who answered said you weren't there anymore."

"I'm not, they moved me to the main office in City Hall. And about my uncle, never listen to him. You know how dramatic he is."

"So wait, stop. I'm confused. What's going on?" I asked.

"Gabriel didn't tell you?"

"Tell me what?"

"Wow, I thought he'd tell you something like this," she said. "Anyway, he gave the city a multimillion dollar grant to begin improvements on the South End of Canyon Cove. One of the stipulations of the grant was that the person leading it has to be a lifelong resident and have the required education in planning. People at work are saying I must be banging him because I was the only person who fit the bill perfectly."

She laughed as she dug into her messenger bag and pulled out a stapled booklet. Flipping through some pages, she finally stopped and turned it around to show me. It was an architectural sketch of the shops I used to pass on the bus ride, but in the sketch, they had been restored. On the corner of the sketch were the words 'Drawing by Gideon Kohl'.

"This outlines the entire plan. The idea is to restore the stores and the gym and to provide grants to the homeowners to make improvements on their homes. We want to get new businesses in the South End and breathe new life into the area. You have no idea how excited I am."

Time flew as Becca and I talked and caught up on the past week. I couldn't believe Gabriel hadn't told me anything about the grant to fix up the South End, but I was proud of him for doing it. As we left Mirabella's, Becca pointed to a new boutique a few doors down.

"Have you been in there yet? I think they just opened," she said.

"No, let's go in."

The store had an old-fashioned look to it with pale pink fabric wallpaper and bronze accents. A woman with grey hair pulled into a large bun smiled as we entered.

"Let me know if there's anything I can help you with," she said.

The store had a little bit of everything: clothes, books, home accessories, and a small jewelry area. We walked around looking at everything until I stopped at the jewelry case, where a silver necklace with a tiny seashell caught my eye.

"Oh, I have to get this for Wendy. She loves the beach. It's her and Gabriel's special daddy-daughter thing. I know she'd love this," I said.

"Things still good between you and the kid?" Becca asked.

"Yeah, she's great. We talk all the time and I've been going out with her to get ready for her visit to her mom. The three of us have dinner together every night and then after he puts Wendy to bed, he still comes over to spend some time with me at the apartment. He always leaves by midnight. I think it's so sweet he wants to make sure he's there in case she has a bad dream. Everything is just perfect. It really is."

"I'm glad, you deserve it and you seem happy."

"What about you? Are you dating anyone?"

"Me?" she said with a laugh. "You know me, I don't want anything serious. I don't have the time anyway."

As I paid for the necklace, I got a text from Gabriel.

Gabriel: *Wendy and I went to the bookstore. Ready to leave work? We can get an early dinner.*

Me: *I'm with Becca. We had dessert at Mirabella's.*

Gabriel: *Guess my secret is out. I'll be by in a few to pick you up. We can take Becca back to City Hall for her truck.*

After dropping Becca off, I turned to Gabriel and tilted my head to the side. He gave me a big shit-eating grin but didn't say anything.

"Did I miss something?" Wendy asked.

"We both did," I said. "Your father gave a grant to restore the South End and put Miss Becca in charge of it."

"Oh, that? I knew about that. Uncle Gideon told me."

"So I'm the only one who didn't know?"

Wendy shrugged. "I guess so."

"I'm always the last to know."

"I wanted it to be a surprise," Gabriel said. "Xander and I are planning a benefit at the Boone Art Gallery for it. I was going to tell you about it then."

"So Ashley knows too?"

Gabriel laughed. "Probably," he said, taking my hand.

"I am really out of the loop," I said, laughing. "I think it's really great. That area needs all the help it can get."

"It's been left to rot for too long. Going back there after all the time I had been away, I realized I couldn't just let it continue. I had to figure out how to make the South End better."

"It'll be great, it really will be. I'm sure of it," I said.

Chapter Sixteen

Gabriel

Stan drove the car through the main terminal and out towards the private jets. I didn't own my own jet. I considered it a waste since I didn't travel often. My plan had been to rent a jet to fly to Phoenix, but I was persuaded into doing something else.

The car stopped and I helped Cassie and Wendy out while Stan grabbed our bags. Just outside the hangar was a sleek white jet with 'Boone' painted in navy blue across the tail. Cassie's brow wrinkled as I took her and Wendy's hands and began walking towards the plane.

"Boone?" she asked. "I know you've been doing some work with him, but I thought you were renting a plane."

"I was going to, but he had a better idea," I said.

"Better idea? What do you mean?"

"You'll see."

I let Cassie climb the steps onto the plane ahead of Wendy and me. As she entered the plane, she stopped in the doorway and turned to me, smiling.

"Ashley!" she said as she ran further into the plane. "What are you doing here? I thought you left for Hawaii a few days ago."

As she hugged Ashley, Wendy and I entered the cabin. Wendy put her backpack down on a tan leather seat then went over to say hello to Jacob, who was sitting on the floor with a toy train. Xander was sitting in a seat in the middle of the cabin. He was wearing a grey suit similar to what he wore the other times we met, a big difference from my jeans and polo shirt.

"You really didn't have to delay your vacation," I said.

"It was only a few days and it's a long flight. I thought it would be nice to break it up with some company."

"Did you tell Ashley we were doing this?"

"No, I figured it would be a nice surprise for her, too. Besides, I didn't think she'd be able to keep it from Cassie since they talk pretty often."

After the plane took off, I moved over to where Wendy was seated, reading a book. Her backpack was open on the seat beside her with her bear's head sticking out of it. I was still having a hard time with her being away, but I tried to convince myself that three days was nothing. Between the fight tomorrow night, having a couple of days with Cassie all to myself, and Wendy being with Dakota, I was torn over how slowly or quickly I wanted the days to go by.

"How are you doing, sweetie? Are you sure you're ready for this?" I asked.

She put her book on her lap and turned to look at me. "I'm good," she said. "I brought some books in case I get bored, but the last time we spoke, Mom said she had a lot of things planned for us to do."

Despite how many times I had told her to call Dakota Mom, it stung hearing her finally use the word without correcting herself.

"I'm glad you're looking forward to it. Just remember if you need me, I'm only an hour away. Call me and I'll drop everything to come get you."

"I know, Daddy, but it's going to be different this time. And it's only three days."

***

I had arranged for a car to take us from the airport to Casa Grande, about an hour south of Phoenix. Once we hit the highway, Cassie opened her bag and pulled out a small gift-wrapped box and handed it to Wendy.

"I got this for you a few weeks ago," Cassie said. "I wanted to wait to give it to you now."

"Really? You got me something?" Wendy said, her eyes lighting up.

I didn't know what the gift was. She hadn't told me anything about it, but I was touched that she thought of giving Wendy something. And by the look on Wendy's face, I knew that no matter what it was, she would love it.

Wendy quickly unwrapped the box and crumpled the paper into a ball. She lifted the lid off the box and squealed like she did whenever she got really excited. I tried to see what the gift was, but Wendy dropped the box on her lap and hugged Cassie tightly before I could get a look at it.

"Put it on me," Wendy said, handing the box back to Cassie.

Wendy turned so her back faced Cassie and pulled up her ponytail. Cassie took the delicate silver necklace out of the box and put it around Wendy's neck. Wendy picked up the small seashell dangling from the necklace and showed it to me.

"Look, Daddy! Just like what we collect when we go to the beach. Thank you, Cassie. I love it! I'm never taking it off."

The beach was something Wendy and I always did together since she was a baby. Dakota hated the beach so even when she was still around, our beach days were something I cherished.

As the car steered through the old town, I tried to brace myself for seeing Dakota. I hoped she really was better. I wanted her to be better, but deep down I didn't think I could trust her.

We pulled up in front of a small, one-story, tan plastered house. The yard was covered with rocks and a couple of tired, dried shrubs tilted towards the cement driveway. A beat up old Mustang sat in front of the garage.

"Stay here," I said to Cassie. "I'll only be a few minutes."

She nodded then turned to Wendy and kissed her cheek.

"The necklace looks beautiful on you," Cassie said. "I'll miss you, but have a great time, okay?"

"I'll miss you too," Wendy said before hugging Cassie.

I grabbed Wendy's bags out of the trunk and as we started walking towards the door, a large dog barked aggressively from inside. Wendy stopped for a minute, her eyes wide.

"Are you okay?" I asked.

"Yes, I just...it startled me."

She rubbed the strap of her backpack on her shoulder and I knew she was wishing she had her bear in her arms. Despite how mature she always acted, it was times like these that I saw my little girl again.

"If anything happens, or even if you're just not happy or comfortable here, you let me know and I'll pick you up."

She nodded as she stared at the front door.

"You charged your phone, right?"

"Yes, it's charged. I'm ready," she said.

She reached for me, and I picked her up and hugged her tight before kissing her cheek. As I set her back on the ground, she started nervously playing with the silver seashell around her neck.

Yelling came from inside the house and then the dog went quiet. The front door opened and Dakota, dressed in a flowing print dress, opened the door.

"There you are," she said. "I was wondering when you were going to get here."

She stepped forward and awkwardly hugged Wendy. Then she bent down and picked up the seashell from around her neck.

"Hmm, we'll buy you something nice while you're here this weekend," she said. "Maybe some turquoise."

"This is nice," Wendy said.

Dakota shrugged. "If you say so. Come inside and I'll introduce you to Samson. Don't worry, he's all bark."

Dakota turned and walked back into the house. It was just like her to control every aspect of the conversation. I wasn't surprised that she didn't speak to me, and I didn't care. It saved me from saying something I might regret in front of Wendy.

Wendy hesitated for a moment and looked up at me. I put my hand on her shoulder and mentally told her to not go.

"I love you, Wendy," I said, thinking about the newborn I held in my arms nine years ago.

"I love you too, Daddy. I brought my charger, so don't worry."

Wendy went into Dakota's house and I turned back to the car where Cassie was waiting. I didn't want to speak. This was the weakest and most vulnerable that I had ever felt. I pulled my phone out of my pocket and turned the volume higher.

"She'll be alright," Cassie whispered.

As the car left Dakota's, Cassie put her arms around me. I thought about the time Cassie and I had been together and the effect she already had on Wendy. I pulled her tight against me, feeling her soft body against mine. She was right, Wendy would be alright.

It was at that moment that I realized I wanted to spend the rest of my life with Cassie.

Chapter Seventeen

Cassie

The next day, Gabriel went to the venue to check on the cage and make sure everything was ready for the fight that night. Since I had some time to myself, I decided to give my mother a call.

"Hello?" my mom said.

"Hi, Mom."

"Who is this?"

"It's Cassie."

"Cassie who? I used to know a Cassie, she was my daughter, but I don't know what happened to her."

"Give me a break, Mom. I just spoke to you three days ago."

"See what I mean? We used to talk everyday."

"Okay, you got me there, happy?"

"Yes, I take great pride in my ability to make you feel guilty," she said, laughing.

"Well, you could've called me, you know."

"I've been busy," she said.

"Oh? I know what that means. You met someone, didn't you?"

"Maybe. I'm just taking him for a test drive. I haven't decided if I'm keeping him."

"Please don't tell me about your test driving him, Mom."

"You really do take all the fun out of it. You get that from your father."

"Yes, yes, only the good stuff came from you."

"No, your father was a good man. The one who raised you, I mean." Mom's voice was uncharacteristically soft. My father had died ten years ago after a long illness. My mother never really got over it.

"Mom, let it go. I miss Dad too, but it's time you moved on. Remember what you told me about us Monroe girls? You can't keep that bottled up. And I'm sure Dad would have wanted you to be happy."

"You're right, Cassie. When you're right, you're right. He was a good man and if it was me, I'd hope your dad would still be getting some."

"Oh, Mom! Did you have to go there?"

"What? That's what I would want. That's what good people deserve. Unlike that sperm donor louse who knocked me up then vanished. *That* father of yours can go to hell."

"Okay, Mother, I don't need a history of my birth."

"Speaking of birth, did you meet Dakota?"

"No, I stayed in the car. From what I've heard, she's enough drama on her own."

"How's Gabriel taking it? My biggest fear was that your birth father would appear out of nowhere and try to take you. That's why I gave you my last name. I didn't want anything to do with him."

"Well, I think he's okay. He was upset yesterday when we dropped her off, but he's been keeping himself busy with the event tonight."

"You know how you can take his mind off of things, right? Remember you're a Monroe," she said.

"Ugh, please. Can't I have a normal conversation with you?"

"This is normal. I'm sure you talk to your friends about that stuff."

"You are not my friend, Mom. I love you, but trust me, learning about the birds and the bees was enough."

"Those bees are pretty kinky, aren't they?" she said with a laugh.

"I'll call you in a couple of days, okay?"

"Alright, honey. Have fun! Don't do anything I wouldn't do."

"Please don't say that. I hate that that leaves off almost nothing," I teased. "Do me a favor and call your new friend. Go out to eat with him or something. I think it'll be good for you."

"Okay, for you I will. And I promise to spare you the details."

"Thanks. I love you."

"I love you, pumpkin."

As I hung up the phone, Gabriel burst into the room and paced the floor as he typed frantically into his phone. His jaw was clenched and I knew something had happened.

"What's going on?" I asked. "Is everything okay?"

"I have to go. Wendy called. She's at the bus station."

"The bus station?"

"Yes, in Casa Grande. I told her to stay there. I have to pick her up. I'm not sure when I'll be back. I'm going to give Dakota a piece of my mind."

"No, you're not going without me," I said.

He stopped pacing and turned towards me, looking at me for the first time since he walked in.

"I know you're upset," I said. "You have every right to be upset, but that anger isn't going to help you if you confront Dakota. You need to calm down. Don't let Wendy see you like this."

He walked over to me and touched my chin as he nodded. "You're right. I need to calm down. Otherwise nothing good will come from this," he said before he kissed me. "I'm glad you're here with me. I need you here with me."

"Let's go. You can tell me everything on the way."

Gabriel had arranged for a rental car and it was waiting for us outside of the hotel. He gave me his phone with the directions to the bus station and started driving.

"Tell me what happened," I said.

"That damn Dakota, that's what happened," he growled. He gritted his teeth then glanced over at me before letting out a deep breath. "I was talking to some people when she called. She sounded really upset, but she wouldn't say what happened, just that she left."

"Where's Dakota? Does she know Wendy's gone?"

"I don't know. My guess is she doesn't know."

"Have you called her?"

"I don't want to speak to her. I just want to get my daughter and make sure she's alright."

"Okay," I said, touching his hand.

He opened his fingers and closed them over mine. Other than the directions I gave him, we drove in silence. Deep down we both knew Wendy was all right. She was resourceful enough to get to the bus station. But that a nine-year-old felt it was better to do that than stay with her mother meant something must have gone wrong.

I didn't know Dakota, so I had no idea what could have happened. On the other hand, Gabriel did. And I could see by the way his jaw clenched and unclenched that he was going through the possibilities.

Less than an hour later, Gabriel stopped the car in front of the bus station and without a word, he ran inside. I followed and as I entered the small waiting area with rows of seats, Wendy leapt into her father's arms and buried her face into his shoulder.

"Are you okay?" Gabriel whispered.

Wendy nodded and turned to me, her eyes red and swollen from crying. She pointed to her backpack and I gave it to her, but she didn't say anything else.

I grabbed her bag and we walked back to the car. Gabriel put the bag in the trunk and as I reached to open the car's front door, Wendy tugged at my shirt and looked at me with pleading eyes.

"You want me to sit in the back?" I asked.

She nodded, so I got in the back and she slid in beside me. I rummaged through my bag to find a tissue for her and found a squished package of Kleenex at the bottom.

"Do you need a tissue?" I asked.

Wendy grabbed the package and then wrapped her arms around me. I held her close as she cried and stroked her hair like my mother used to when I was upset. Just as I knew when Gabriel didn't want to talk, I knew Wendy needed some time, too.

Back at the hotel, we went straight to the room. It was a large suite with a king size bedroom behind closed doors. Wendy sat on the couch and Gabriel kneeled in front of her.

"Are you hurt?" he asked.

"No," she whispered.

"Does your mother know you left?"

She shook her head.

"Where is she?"

"I don't know," she whispered.

Gabriel rose to his feet and went into the bedroom, slamming the door behind him. I sat beside Wendy and put my arm around her. Through the closed door, we could hear Gabriel on the phone.

"It's Gabriel," he said. "Where's Wendy?"

Silence.

"Oh? She's at your home? Then where are you?" he asked.

Silence.

"Really. You decided to go away with your boyfriend."

Silence.

"Wendy wasn't alone? She had Samson? Your dog? You left a nine year old alone with your crazy dog?"

Silence.

"Oh I see, you invited her, but she didn't want to go. You know what, Dakota? You can forget about ever seeing Wendy again."

Silence. Then SMASH!

Wendy and I jumped as something crashed against the wall. We waited quietly, staring at the bedroom door until Gabriel finally opened it. He looked at us calmly and smiled.

"I need to call room service. The lamp threw itself against the wall," he said. He sat down next to Wendy, and I pulled my arm away as he pulled her close. "I'm sorry about what happened."

"It's my fault," she said. "I thought it was going to be different."

"It's not your fault," Gabriel said. "She's your mother, it's her fault for not taking care of you."

Her hand went up and pulled the silver seashell out from inside her shirt, stroking it nervously. She turned back towards me, the shell still between her fingers.

"I want Cassie to move in with us," she said.

***

After Wendy fell asleep in the bed, Gabriel and I went out to the balcony and looked at the city lights. Room service came earlier and cleaned up the lamp and fixed the pullout sofa bed for Gabriel to sleep on.

"If you want to check on the fights, I don't mind staying here with her," I said.

"No, they don't need me. I'd rather be here with you anyway. I'm sorry everything turned out the way it did."

"Don't apologize for being passionate and caring about your daughter."

"It's not that," he said. "I had plans for this weekend, for us."

"Plans? You didn't tell me you planned anything. Why do you keep wanting to surprise me?" I asked, laughing nervously.

"Because I wanted it to be special. You are special to me, Cassie. And I want everything I do to remind you of that and how much I love you. The time we've been together has been the best time of my life, and every day I fall in love with you even more." He held his finger up and tapped his phone then waited with it by his ear. "It's Gabriel Kohl. Do it now."

Gabriel put his arm around me and pointed towards the arena. A small light blinked above the arena, like a plane flying too low. Suddenly red words appeared and flashed across and I realized it wasn't a plane, it was a blimp.

Cassie, will you marry me?

The words floated across the blimp. I had to let the words float past several times as the meaning sank in. Gabriel made me speechless again.

Cassie, he's waiting...

I laughed and turned to Gabriel. "How are you doing this?" I asked.

"I told you, I made plans. And, as you can see it spelled out in front of you, I'm still waiting for your answer."

"Yes. The answer is yes."

"She said yes," he spoke into the phone before he put it away.

Gabriel swept me into his arms and kissed me deeply. I wrapped my arms around him as he held me close and gently swayed to the music coming up from the hotel lobby. As he spun me around, I noticed the blimp again.

She said YES!

"Did I surprise you?" he asked.

"You did. Now can we stop with the surprises?"

"I promise, no more surprises." He pulled a small box out of his pocket, bent down on one knee, and held the box up to me. "Okay, this is the last surprise."

He pulled back the lid, and inside was a simple round diamond solitaire. As I took the box, Gabriel removed the ring and and took my hand.

"I was going to propose and ask you to move in, but Wendy beat me to it," he said.

"Actually, and I know you might find this hard to believe, but I'm a little old-fashioned."

"Cassie, if you're saying what I think you are, Vegas is just a plane ride away."

Epilogue
Cassie

Three Months Later

With Becca's new job and everything planned for the South End, she was able to buy the building her apartment was in. I had been helping her on the weekends with some things while Gabriel and Wendy had their daddy-daughter time together.

Ashley had told me she and her friends were meeting at Mirabella's Café for dinner and they wanted me to join them. I knew they would love Becca too, so I convinced her to go along. As Becca and I entered the restaurant, she turned to me with a nervous look on her face.

"Are you sure it's okay that I'm here," she asked. "What if I'm not dressed right?"

"We're both in jeans, I'm sure we're fine. They're not going to care, they're really nice and funny too. And of course it's okay that you're here. Besides, I want you to meet my cousin."

Ashley was already there, seated at the same round table as last time. Next to her were Jackie and Tara. Everyone was dressed casually. Someone entered right behind us, and I turned around to see who it was.

"Oh good, I was hoping I wasn't the last to get here," Deborah said. "I'm always late."

"No, Deborah, you're last, as usual," Ashley teased. "Samantha isn't coming. She's not feeling well."

"When's she due?" I asked.

"Any day now," Ashley said.

As Becca, Deborah, and I sat down, Jackie leaned forward as she looked me over.

"What?" I asked. "Did I already spill something?"

"I'm checking for new jewelry," she said, grinning.

"You mean like this?" Becca asked as she raised my left hand.

Jackie grabbed my hand and nodded appreciatively at the diamond solitaire.

"Exactly like that," Jackie said.

"See, that's why we have these dinners," Deborah said. "I talk to Ashley all the time and she never told me you got engaged."

"I'm very good at keeping secrets," Ashley said as she smiled at me.

"You're the best," I said. "But enough about me. Deborah, last time you mentioned Mr. Sexy. Did you ever find out his name?" I asked.

"I did! It's William King, and he's pretty amazing," Deborah said. "But that's all I'm saying. I don't want to jinx anything. You know me, I'm just going with the flow. No regrets."

"No regrets," Tara grumbled. "I wish I could say that."

"Mason still?" Ashley asked.

Tara nodded and sighed.

"Give him another chance" Ashley said. "You said he asked you out, I thought you were going to go."

"It's complicated. I was going to go, but then I cancelled," Tara said. "And then he asked again so I said yes again."

"And let me guess, then you cancelled. Again," Ashley said.

"You got that right. You have no idea how bad that man hurt me, but every time I'm near him I can't say no."

"It was years ago, Tara. He was your first love," Ashley said. "He's a sweet man and I can tell there's still something there. I wish you'd give him a second chance."

"Speaking of chances, what about you, Jackie? You're oddly quiet," Deborah said.

Jackie shrugged. "Nothing's going on with me. I'm still waitressing while I finish school."

"But what about Brent Winslow?" Ashley asked. "You know Samantha wanted me to nudge you about him."

"I thought I caught a break with Samantha not here," Jackie said as she looked across the table at Becca and grinned. "I have too much going on to date. Besides, we have fresh meat here today. I'm sure she's much more interesting than me. What's your story, Becca? Has Cassie's luck rubbed off on you?"

"Hmm…maybe, but not in the way I think you mean," Becca said. "Gabriel created a grant which gave me a great job, and I just bought a house. I'm really with you, Jackie, I have too much going on. The last thing I need now is another distraction."

"I will drink to that," Jackie said, raising her glass.

"Well, take it from me," I said. "Love comes along when you least expect it."

***

Dinner with the girls went by quickly. It was great catching up with them and talking about whatever came to mind, but as I noticed a familiar black limo pulling up to the curb outside, I realized how much I had missed Gabriel.

I said my goodbyes and we made plans to meet again soon. As I stepped outside, Stan opened the car door for me. I slid in beside Wendy, and Gabriel leaned over to give me a kiss. They were both still dressed for the beach.

"Home, Sir?" Stan asked from the driver's seat.

"Yes," Gabriel said to Stan, then turned to me. "So what did you talk about? Did you tell them we got married?"

"No, I think they were surprised enough I got engaged, can you imagine what would've happened if I said we got married the next day? You know me, I don't like being the center of attention."

"Yes, I know. That's what you said when we talked about Vegas."

"I just wanted the people who really mattered to me there. And they were," I said as I smiled at Gabriel and Wendy. "I still can't believe we got my mother, Becca, Ashley and her family, and Gideon out there so quickly."

"Anything for you, Cassie," he said as he squeezed my hand.

"How was the beach?" I asked.

"It was great!" Wendy said. "We made a sand castle and I found a shell just like my necklace." She pulled a small seashell out of the pail and held it up next to her pendant. "See?"

"That's great!" I said. "It sounds like you had a great time."

"We did," she said. "You should come with us next time."

"But I thought the beach was for daddy-daughter time," I said.

"Well, maybe we can make it family time," Wendy said, smiling.

I looked over at Gabriel, and he nodded. "We would both love to have you there."

"I'd love that too," I said, hugging Wendy.

As I sat back and listened to Wendy and Gabriel talk about their day, I realized that what I had said inside was true. Love comes along when you least expected it. Less than a year ago, I moved to Canyon Cove with dreams of finding a job, never expecting that I would end up with a gorgeous man who loved me and a daughter that I had come to love like my own.

I couldn't believe how lucky I was, and sometimes I still had to pinch myself to make sure I wasn't dreaming. I thought back to all those times when I doubted Gabriel and shook my head, a slight grin tugging on my mouth. Ashley was right – sometimes taking a leap of faith was worth it.

About The Author

Liliana Rhodes is a New York Times and USA Today Bestselling Author who writes Contemporary and Paranormal Romance. Blessed with an overactive imagination, she is always writing and plotting her next stories. She enjoys movies, reading, photography, and listening to music. After growing up in New Jersey, Liliana now lives in California with her husband, son, two dogs who are treated better than some people, and two parrots who plan to take over the world.

Connect Online

www.LilianaRhodes.com

www.facebook.com/AuthorLilianaRhodes

Made in the USA
Middletown, DE
28 April 2018